The Wishcharmer

Saga

Volume One

Beginnings

Hello there!
This is your Grand-Son!
Vance! The Weird-looking one!
I hope you enjoy this book and
the words that are in it.
I Miss you Grandpa, and Grandma, too!
Anyways, enjoy! Love you!

Vance Smith

Also by

Vance Smith

JACK LANTERN ...BRAINS...

JACK LANTERN 2

TALES BY

LANTERN-LIGHT

Shadow Mountain
And the Secret
Of the Gatekeepers

Shadow Mountain
And the Ghostly
Abbey
December 2015

Cavrey

Buri's Retirment Home •
• Dwel

•Durjen

Far away, there is a place where magic lives. Where it governs the lives and destinies of every living thing. Controlled by masters of the great magic realms, the world is observed, and watched over by ancient practitioners from the Djinn, the Sorcerers, and the Goluems...

Most mysterious of the Magic Tribes, however, are the Wishcharmers. Untrusted by all, it is unclear whether this shadowy group stands ready to save the world, or destroy it...

The Wishcharmer Saga

Vance Smith

1st

Passage

Rajhu's Lamp

Vance Smith

1st

Passage

Rajhu's Lamp

Vance Smith

1st

Passage

Rajhu's Lamp

The Wishcharmer Saga: Beginnings

'How long have you had *this* piece?'

The old man looked up, taking his gaze off the gleaming gold form of the lamp. His pale eyes wandered for a moment, finally settling on Rajhu as he tipped the lamp this way and that, letting the metal catch the light in different ways.

'Huh... Oh, I... I can't remember, to be truthful...'

Rajhu smiled.

A crowd had gathered around his booth. The

bystanders were watching with rapt attention as he surveyed the discarded relics they brought. It was a national roadshow: A place where people brought things, for the hope they might be worth some grand sum, and whisk them away from their dreary existence, planting them firmly in the earth of the opulent.

It was a place of hope, and of desperation.

Rajhu nodded, looking at the lamp again. He brought a hand back, scrubbing the fake moustache that was firmly glued to his upper lip. It was itching, but there was simply nothing to be done about it, at this point. Too many people had seen him today. Too many of the other inspectors had chatted with him, and discussed his methodology.

Now, he would have to suffer a little longer. Soon, the day would end, and he could take what he had gained, and be done with it. Looking at the lamp, he smiled again. Such a find could take him far. If only he could convince this man to part with it.

A simple con, but an effective one.

'I can't recall where I picked it up,' the old man

The Wishcharmer Saga: Beginnings

was saying. He rubbed his white beard and shook his head. 'It's as if I've always had it. I suppose I was just curious. Like all these folks, I wondered if it was just junk, or... or something more...'

Something more, indeed! Rajhu let himself laugh. He reached out, patting the man on the shoulder and setting the lamp down on the little table in front of him.

'A wonder, indeed, sir. It's a magnificent piece.'

'I've always thought so...'

'These intricate carvings, you see?' he pointed at the widest part of the lamp. 'They're quite wondrous, correct?'

'Yes, very beautiful.'

'And sadly, they are the undoing of this whole thing!'

'I'm sorry?'

'Oh, think nothing of it... It's a sad example, but one I see more often than not. Interesting pieces, wonderful workmanship... but forgeries, usually.' He bobbled his head, leaning across the small table. 'You know, there are a lot of untrustworthy people running about Ideji, these days. I can't tell you the amount of times I've been swindled. It's a time of con men and forgers, my friend. Like this lamp, they make you believe in something, but it's nothing more than an empty vessel.'

The old man's shoulders sagged. 'A forgery... It's strange... I've always had it with me, as long as I can remember. I felt it was important. Like, like it held some secret to my life, and my purpose.'

'Perhaps sentimental value is important, my friend,' Rajhu smiled. 'But, in the times we live in, sentiment weighs you down. It's no good. Waste of time.' He patted the lamp, looking at the intricate carvings in the thick, heavy, gold.

'And besides all this,' he frowned. 'The whole thing is actually lead. Not gold...'

The old man stared at him in disbelief. He couldn't blame him. It was a far fetched idea. The weight was right, the feel was right. It was obviously gold. But Rajhu couldn't let him continue to believe that.

'Lead?'

Rajhu nodded. 'Mmhmm. Afraid so. It's a very

naughty process. They weave components of fools gold into boiling lead. Diabolical. Charlatans. Bleeding false alchemists.'

'And so...' the man slumped. 'It is worthless.'

Rajhu leaned back in his chair abruptly. 'To you, yes. But to me?' He smiled. 'It's a very interesting piece, sir... I... I would like to buy it from you, if you are willing. These are troubled times, you know. Gold is more useful than lead, wouldn't you say?'

The man nodded, but looked unconvinced. Sentiment. That was what held him back. Sentiment had robbed Rajhu of many good finds in the past. He was insistent that today would not be a repeat of such things.

'I would offer you... fifteen gold Flank for the piece, sir. It's a good solid price,' he added, bobbling his head.

'Fifteen?' the man wondered.

He wasn't sold.

'Because it interests me, and I'd like to track down the scoundrels that made it...' Rajhu checked his purse. He hadn't much money left. The day had seen him run this ploy a few times. He had gained several worthwhile properties... but had run out nearly all of his gold.

'I would go as high as twenty-five.' He winced as he said the words. That would end it, for sure. He couldn't make a higher offer than that, and if the man gave in, he would be without money. He still hadn't eaten today...

'Twenty-five gold?' the man laughed, his lips curling into a tentative smile.

'It's a very interesting piece, as I've said.'

The man rubbed at his beard, considering. Looking up, he nodded slowly, extending his hand. 'These are troubled times, indeed. Gold is more important than sentiment. Yes?'

Rajhu sighed in relief, letting himself smile as well. 'Too right, sir... Too right!'

The Wishcharmer Saga: Beginnings

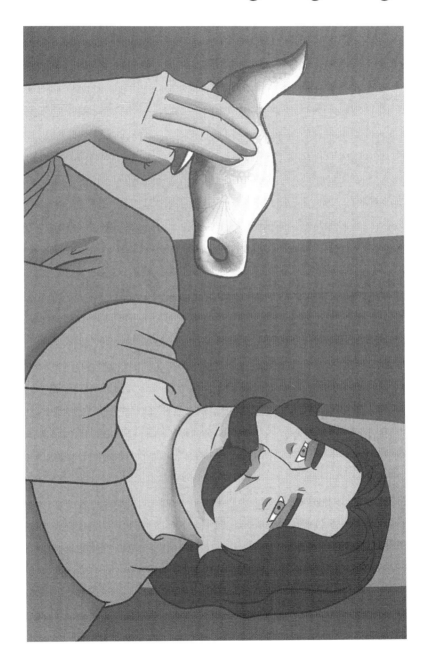

Vance Smith

2

The column of guards marched past, their spears barely wavering as they moved. Their loose tan pants ruffled in the evening breeze, but Rajhu had his eyes on their black breastplates, and the gleaming scimitars at their hips. The guardsmen of king Serafa were not to be trifled with. And Rajhu had trifled, indeed.

He snaked his way into an alley, the sandstone buildings rising up on either side of him. The sun may have been setting, but it was still hot. That was the problem with this country. It was always hot outside. And if it wasn't, it was far too cold. Night was the only relief from the inhuman heat, and day was the only escape from the frigid cold.

Grabbing the large bag that hung over his shoulder, he groped desperately, until his hands wrapped around the shape of the lamp. The solid gold, ancient lamp. He still couldn't believe his little confidence scam had turned out such a wonder. With this prize, things would change for him. He reached up to his face and peeled away the bushy moustache. Relief washed over him as the appliance fell away. He scratched his lip, and sighed openly.

It had been a good day.

The sound of marching soldiers echoed through the streets, and Rajhu picked up his pace, weaving through the alleys as fast as his feet would carry him. It was late, and soon the city gates would close. If he had any hope for his future, he needed to be out of the city before that happened.

Skidding around a corner, the alleyway opened

up, revealing a wide street, lined on both sides with open shop faces. Men and women still mulled about, but the scene was far from what it would be in the morning, or afternoon.

The clang of metal on metal rang out above half hearted calls for people to come see this or that, to buy now, while prices were low. It drummed above all of this, and Rajhu's eyes settled onto the form of a young man, slaving away over red metal and anvil.

Smiling, Rajhu hurried forward, walking up to the lad and ruffling his tidy brown hair.

The boy jerked backward, looking up with anger and alarm. His features softened when he realised who it was.

'Oh, it's you...'

'Good evening to you, too, Will.'

The boy wiped his brow, drawing sweat and soot across his already dirty face. His complexion was sullied by the day's work, but Rajhu knew the boy to be very fair. Much fairer than his own people from the mountains and valleys of Ohmi. Will was a child of the north countries. Rajhu didn't remember their names, but knew they existed. Will was an orphan of them, as Rajhu was of his own country.

'I have this!' Rajhu insisted, digging in his bag and producing the gold lamp.

Will stopped his work again and looked at the thing, his eyes going wide.

'With such an amount of gold, you won't have to work anymore. We can get out of this dreadful country and go somewhere nice.'

'Put it away!' Will insisted, striding forward and pushing the lamp hastily back into Rajhu's satchel. 'Who'd you con *this* off of, anyway?'

Rajhu frowned. 'I paid the man, Will.'

'Yeah... you gave him a pittance, Raj. It's not honest. What I do here...' he opened his arms, then let them fall to his sides. 'It's honest...'

'And you make the finest swords in the land, Will. A true testament to the art of Smithing. But this isn't where you belong. You're no apprentice Blacksmith. You're a *master!* A *swordsman!*'

'And I'm not a con man, Raj... Listen, I know we've been through a lot, but I just can't deal with this conning business. That's why I got the job here in the first place. So we could earn some honest money.'

'We don't need honest money, Will! We need money. Period. How do you think the King gained his riches. I guarantee you, it wasn't honestly. So we take a little from dishonest people. I pay them a part of the worth, and they are happier for it.'

'But when does it end?'

'Tonight! Tonight it ends. Will, you are my only friend, yeah? Tonight, we are finally rich men. Tonight, we are freemen! Now, let's start living like it!'

Will smiled. 'Freemen, hey? Okay, I'm not gonna lie, I like the sound of that.'

'Exactly, my boy! Exactly! We can do whatever we want!'

Will walked past the forge, folding his hands across his chest. 'So... we could go to the north countries?'

'Of course!'

'Try and find my parents?'

'Will, I'm your friend. I would be honoured to help

you find them.'

'Could we... start our own country?'

Rajhu smiled. 'It's been a dream of mine for as long as I've been alive. You know that!'

'Can we call the country Willtopia?'

Rajhu sagged. 'That is honestly the worst name I have ever heard.'

Will laughed. 'I thought it was pretty good!'

There was a sudden commotion somewhere behind him, and Rajhu heard someone calling out. Turning, he could see the column of soldiers walking through the marketplace. The Captain at the head of the group pointed toward Rajhu, his scimitar drawn.

'Stop there, thief!'

'We can talk about names and such later. Right now, we need to be getting out of the city.'

Will's shoulders fell. 'What have you done now, Raj?'

He scrunched up his face, bobbling his head. 'I may have taken the King for a walk. I may have told him I was his lost son. I may have told him that my Mother was sick, and dying. I may have told him I needed... two thousand Flank. He might have given it to me...'

'You *have* been busy!' Will grimaced.

The column of soldiers rushed forward, falling on them in a moment. Will kicked out, catching the Captain in the leg; he sputtered a curse, and crashed to the ground.

A spear darted out, and Raj stepped to the side as it whistled past his face. He grabbed the shaft and pulled it free from the hands of his attacker, ramming the butt into his face. Blood spurted from the man's nose, and he fell backward, just as Raj rammed the back of the spear into his breastplate, sending him sprawling to the ground.

More soldiers rushed in, and as they did, the Captain climbed to his feet, growling as he brandished his scimitar. He whirled, turning to face Raj, his teeth bared. He raised his sword, stepping forward. The blade came down, but before it could cleave Raj's skull in two, Will stepped between them, his own sword raised. The width of the blade took the impact, and he pushed back, parrying the blow.

The Wishcharmer Saga: Beginnings

The Captain cursed, swinging again, but Will stepped, then brought his sword up, the flat slamming into the side of the Captain's head. He stumbled back, and Will moved again. His sword flashed, and the Captain barked. Metal impacted metal, and Raj saw the man's scimitar clatter to the sandy ground.

Will drove the pommel of his weapon into the man's face and he, like his sword, fell to the ground, unmoving.

Spear men moved in, and Will turned. He batted an attack away with his blade, then slashed upward, clipping the arm of the attacker. The guard stumbled back, and Will charged, bowling over the man, as Rajhu smiled, darting through the crowd of stunned soldiers. Before they could completely register what had happened, Will and Raj were at a full run.

A cry of rage rose up from their ranks, but it was lost to Rajhu as he and Will darted around a corner and immediately began to descend a narrow set of stone stairs. Behind them, Raj glimpsed the trailing attackers, but they burst free from the stairwell onto even ground, and disappeared behind yet another sharp corner.

They ran in spurts, for nearly half of an hour. At long last, Rajhu saw the gates to the mighty city: Two massive wooden doors that raised half the height of the stone walls. The city was known for being near impossible to penetrate, and almost harder to escape - if the need arose.

'Made it!' Will panted, coming to a stop beside Rajhu. 'With time to spare, too! They haven't even started to close the gates, yet!'

As he spoke the words, a great grinding noise split the air. Rajhu gave the boy a whithering glance, and darted forward.

'How was I supposed to know they'd start closing them?' Will protested. 'Hey, you cannot blame me for this!'

They sprinted, and Rajhu felt his legs giving renewed protest. His body was tired, his mind was tired. But they were so incredibly close. Beyond those gates lay freedom the likes of which he hadn't known in years; the likes of which Will had probably *never*

The Wishcharmer Saga: Beginnings

experienced.

Above them, there were cries from the gatehouse. Raj smiled. They were closing on the gates now. The doors still stood halfway open.

An arrow whizzed by him, stabbing into the ground. He cursed.

'They're a little upset, Will!' he called. 'I think I've angered the whole city this time!'

More arrows rained down, but they were crossing under the gatehouse now. Rajhu laughed as they darted through the closing gates, out of the city, and into the open flat expanse beyond. The last flecks of sunlight were fading as the gates closed behind them. Above, there was a host of cursing. He knew they were looking for them, waiting for a chance to pin them both to the ground with their arrows. After such an escape, Raj wouldn't allow himself such an ignominious end. Silently, he lead Will away from the gatehouse. They stayed in the shadow of the city walls, until they were sure the guardsmen had given up. Then they broke away from the wall and started their long journey away from the city, and into the vast unknown.

'You almost got me killed!' Will growled through a smile, hitting Raj hard in the arm.

'I got us out...' he smiled. 'Will... We are freemen, now!' He laughed, twirling around as he kicked up the sand at his feet. 'I knew today was auspicious! What a turn of luck! And it all stems from my crowning achievement...' He reached into his bag, pulling free the golden lamp. 'My lamp... The golden wonder! The signal of our future, Will. This... This is just the beginning, my friend.'

Will laughed. 'You're crazy, Raj...'

Rajhu stopped, peering at his friend through the darkness. The moon burst light onto the desert through the veil of a pale cloud.

'But of course... I'm Raj Heroh. You must have heard of me. Dashing, powerful, the master of a thousand charms and disciplines...'

'And a very lucky con man, too!'

Rajhu laughed. 'Maybe you're right...' he conceded, bobbling his head. 'But tonight, Will, I am Raj. King of the world!'

The Wishcharmer Saga: Beginnings

Will laughed, and Rajhu kissed the lamp delicately before stowing it back in his bag. Tonight was a new beginning. Tonight, truly, he was standing on the edge of greatness. He had left the squalor and the failure behind. His past was dead in the city behind them. Now, the future was as bright as gold.

Rajhu was sure. There was nothing stopping them, now.

Vance Smith

3

The old man clutched his chest as power flooded through his body. He screamed as it arced back on itself and intensified. Somehow, he recognised this power. As it washed over him, memories returned, along with strength. Flesh fell away from him, as well as bones and blood and mortality. He floated off the ground, looking around at the city that hung over him.

Several ghostly beings encircled him, their eyes observing with displeasure. As he floated there, he realised their names, and their purposes.

Vance Smith

'Ferro,' a large ghostly man growled. He folded arms of chorded muscle across his chest. Scars adorned his face, and inky black hair was pulled back from his eyes into a tight ponytail.

'You have been sentenced to five hundred years of penance, for the murder of your charge. Your sentence is now at an end. How do you plead?'

Ferro looked up at the men and women who surrounded him. Something sparked in his mind at their words.

'Murder of my... *charge?*' A smile crept across his face, and he rubbed at his beard. 'Djinn council... At last you free me from my hell. You return my memory to me, and now, I know why there was a burden of sorrow through these last five hundred years... I plead guilty. I ask your forgiveness.'

The man with the ponytail nodded. 'Forgiveness, we grant to you.'

Ferro smiled. 'Then, why have you not returned me to my complete power? Forgiveness dictates that sin is forgotten. Where is my magic? I feel it, but part of it is gone. Missing from my reach!'

The Wishcharmer Saga: Beginnings

'There has been... an incident...' a woman said, cautiously.

'Incident?' Ferro snarled.

'This day... Do you not remember what you did?' a powerful man with a large turban asked.

'What did I do? I...' The memory flashed in Ferro's mind. 'My lamp!'

'Because of greed that still infects your heart, you sold your lamp for gold, Ferro. With it went half of your magic.'

'But I was swindled! I didn't remember the import of the lamp!'

'Yet you sold it, nonetheless!'

'Hebak, please! There must be something you can do!'

The muscular Djinn sighed, looking down at Ferro. 'Your magic now belongs to the man who owns the lamp. He has split your power. Because of this, you, are no longer Djinn. You are less. A half breed. Magi. This is what you have become.'

'A Wishcharmer!' Ferro barked. ' Do you realise what you have done? You've let me fall from grace, from Djinn to Magi... But worse, you've allowed a Wishcharmer to be created!'

'You have allowed it to happen yourself, Ferro!' Hebak growled. 'Perhaps now, you may see the import of these humans. Perhaps now, you will truly know why we punished you.'

'This is sacrilege! You have no right to allow this to happen! We must stop him! Kill the wretch. I can absorb his power, regain what I've lost...'

'We hold no blame in this, nor any part in its consequence... It is what you sold that makes you what you are. What you gave away that allowed the Wishcharmer to form. Greed, like before, is still your undoing.'

'You will return what is mine, Hebak! You will, or I will reign terror on these people. A Wishcharmer will be the least of your worries! I swear it!'

'You are no longer our concern. The sorcerers have been made aware of you. Do not think blood will change what has transpired.'

'I will kill this man! The one who took my lamp! His blood will be on your hands!'

The Wishcharmer Saga: Beginnings

'Do you not remember who we are, Ferro?' Hebak asked. 'We are Djinn! We know of things beyond time!' His voice thundered around Ferro, shaking the city all around him.

'I want what is mine!' he snapped.

'What once was yours, has allowed for something else. The Djinn see him. We are aware of him. And we may yet have use for him... Do not cross us by seeking his death, Ferro. Such an act would bring about a war that you, in your eternities, have not seen the likes of. Not since the founding of the universe has there been such a war. But this man is tied to such a fate. This, we have foreseen. Do not test the will of the Djinn. Even we must answer to higher powers...'

'Curse you all! I will have my power back! I swear to you! If it takes every eternity I have left, I will have it back! And I will make you, and that human-child suffer for this affront! I swear it!'

Hebak nodded. 'Then we shall soon see, what the universe can bear. If war is what you create, Ferro... We shall see what heroes the great power of the universe raises to oppose you...'

Vance Smith

There was a sudden brilliant green flash, and then, Ferro was alone. Comforted in the dark, only by his mission. Warmed in the cold, only by his hatred.

2nd

Passage

The Sorceress

4

It was raining in the great city of Geb. Water poured down from the heavens in great drafts, soaking everything. In the dim morning light, the streets glimmered, illuminated by the magic lanterns that dotted the city. Thousands upon thousands of the devices shone out a heavy orange light.

Gwendolyn Freemont watched from her position, high above the city. She saw the people walking slowly, yet with a curious desire to remain dry. They wandered. That's what it always seemed like. These people she observed simply wandered through their lives. Gwen, on the other hand, had always known what she was to do. Every moment of her life had been scheduled, since the day she was brought here, to Geb.

High above the rest of its inhabitants, Gwen lived in the White Tower - one of the three towers of Geb, each soaring one hundred meters over the city. They were forged by Gwen's master, and she knew each of them well. But here, in the White Tower, is where she liked to be best. It was situated in the centre of Geb, and therefore gave her the best view of the city. The best place to watch the people wander.

Turning from the oval window, Gwen moved back, further into the large circular room. It occupied the entire diameter of the tower. Each level was built in the same fashion, with each floor becoming progressively smaller. Here, near the top of the building, the room wasn't more than five meters across, but it housed a large number of books, a solid oak desk, and a single cupboard, holding her clothes and Sorcerer's Armour.

There was a sudden flash in the centre of the room. Gold light flickered all about, and as it faded, an elderly man replaced the brightness. His wide eyes observed the room, while his thin, long arms patted down his skeletal frame. He wore a white shirt and tie, buried under a black coat that came nearly to his knees. Twitching his nose, all attention was brought to the thin moustache he wore. Long and waxed, it made him look like an old man with giant antennae growing from his top lip.

'Salvidi!' the man declared, throwing his hands out wide.

Gwen smiled, but bowed.

'My child, my child, there has been a great upheaval in the universe... Things have changed, girl!' The man spoke in a thick accent, and a sense of dread bore out from his eyes.

Gwen tilted her head to the side. 'Master Salvidi... slow down. I'm not sure what you're talking about.'

'Gwendolyn! You're a sorceress now. I expect you to know what I'm talking about before I have even said it! Before even I know what I'm talking about! Come now, you must have felt the disturbance... It split its way through the magic like an axe! Something has happened...'

Gwen brushed back her silky, raven hair and shook her head. 'I've felt very little, Master. I've been observing the people.'

'Again? By the stars, how much do these people change from day to day?' He took a few cautious steps toward the window, but waved a hand dismissively before turning back to Gwen.

'No... It simply won't do. You will have to go. Find the source of this disturbance and bring it back to me. Only then, will I be able to fix whatever has been broken.'

He snapped his fingers, a cane appearing in his hands instantly. He nodded, twitching his nose. 'I have decided. Beyond this, I know that the problem resonates from a man. A man carrying a lamp.'

'A lamp?'

'Yes. A lamp which was, only a short time ago, the property of a very dangerous Djinn.'

Gwen furrowed her brow. 'So, what is it you want me to do?'

Salvidi's shoulders slumped. He let his cane slip, and he leaned on it heavily. 'Have I not just told you? Bring this man and his lamp back to me. A Wishcharmer has been created, my dear! Such a thing, it has completely upset the realm of the Djinn, and its ripples are crashing across the universe, affecting all magic! If we are not too careful, if we don't end this line of Wishcharmers before it sets in... Great evils could awaken from the darkest parts of the universe...'

'Master, I...'

'The Salvidi has no time for questions, Gwendolyn! Such is the burden I carry... The greatest Sorcerer in all the world, and not a moment to answer the questions of his only pupil... Be gone! Lest we bring destruction on all these people you love to watch!'

'None of this makes sense!' she insisted.

'Of course it doesn't!' Salvidi barked. 'This is the madness of our world. Whatever Creator forged this universe must have more faith in us than I do. Nothing makes sense anymore, my dear child. Indeed, this Wishcharmer shouldn't exist. It should be *impossible* for him to exist, but the Djinn have told me. They have shown him to me!'

'But I don't even know what a Wishcharmer is! How am I supposed to bring him to you?'

'The man is as unawares as you are, Gwendolyn. That is our only advantage!'

'He doesn't know he is a... a...'

'A Wishcharmer. Yes. We must keep it that way, if at all possible. I can't stress to you enough, my girl, the gravity of this situation. You simply *must* bring him back to me, before the next full moon, or disaster will surely follow...'

There was no arguing with the man. Not when he was like this. Gwen had never seen her Master in such a state. Through all her tutelage, she had never seen him thus. He was manic, and beyond powerful... But never before had she seen her master... *scared*.

He set about the room, gathering her things. With a wave of his cane, he sent her armour and clothing whirling through the air, and into an open travel bag.

'I've never heard of a Wishcharmer before...' she pressed, walking toward the old man, as she clasped her hands behind her back.

'Of course you haven't!' he barked, flicking his cane. The travel bag clasped itself closed and he turned to Gwen, a hard look in his eyes. 'They are not something we like to talk about... Shadows of the past, my dear...'

'...Often turn to visions of the future...' She nodded, completing the old adage. It had been taught to her all of her life. She'd had a different understanding of it's meaning, but perhaps she was mistaken. Perhaps the phrase had meant to speak of this apparent threat. These... Wishcharmers.

Salvidi nodded. 'Something like that...' He looked up, his eyes brightening, a smile lifting the corners of his mouth. 'Now, you will take with you, this cat. Companion, dearest to my heart. He will protect you. He, my dearest Babo...'

His cane snapped through the air once more, and a cat about the size of an ocelot appeared on the ground before her. It looked up, as if considering her, before snorting, and walking past her, to sit by her bag. It tilted its head to the side, looking at her lazily.

Salvidi leaned closer to Gwen. 'You should be leaving now... Babo has little time for wastrels.'

'What?'

'Oh, not you, my dear... not you! But he will go along with you, to make sure you complete your task. The Sorcerer Council has deemed it necessary. I don't mind telling you, they're displeased with the appearance of a Wishcharmer... Displeased, indeed...'

'But I still don't have any idea what this man is. Is he really such a danger that we need to find him, to bring him back to the Sorcerer Council?'

'I should say so, yes... You see... the Wishcharmers are, by far, the most dangerous of the Universal Powers... Dangerous, and unpredictable... Hurry, my child. Babo will explain more of it to you on the road. Time is short. We must stop him, my dear. Such a man could upset the delicate peace of the world. You must find him. Stop him. Bring him back. His life spells war in all the stars. And the kind of war he

Vance Smith

would bring, we are far from ready for...'

5

The heat, oppressive as it was, hung across the sky. It pressed down on Rajhu as he moved. It surged up from the sand as well, trapping him in a vise. He let out a groan of exhaustion as he looked forward, across the unending expanse of sand dunes.

They were no more than half a day's journey from Durjen, the city of sand. He wasn't sure if they were being followed. He'd thought he'd spotted something behind them early in the morning. That had been hours ago, however. The memory seemed distant, and somehow unattainable, like it were on some tall shelf, and he had no way of reaching it to study it more closely.

Shifting the weight of his bag, Rajhu looked across to Will, as the younger boy trudged beside him. There had been nothing much the boy had owned in this world, and yet, he'd left it all behind to come with Rajhu on this journey.

'I am going to die, Will... Leave my corpse for the animals, but bury my lamp somewhere nice...' He slumped to the ground, but the heat of the sand scorched his bare arms, and he scrambled back onto his wobbling legs.

'*Koliba!*' he cursed. 'The desert won't even let a man die in peace!'

Will stopped in his tracks beside Rajhu. Wearily, he looked the man over, shaking his head. 'I haven't seen a road for hours... I thought you said this corridor was used by traders!'

Rajhu rubbed his face, sand rolling over his tanned skin. He shrugged weakly. 'I was told as much by the merchants... But it's only a two day journey between Durjen and the border. We will survive... I think.'

'We'd be lucky to survive another hour, Raj...'

He clicked his tongue. 'You're negative, my friend. Very... negative...'

They struggled forward, climbing a tall dune as the heat crashed against them from all sides. Rajhu could feel his insides churning, for water, food, and rest. But none of those things were within his power. The water was nearly all gone, as was the food. Rest couldn't come, if they hoped to make it to water. No.... As much as he wanted to give up, he couldn't!

As they crested the top of the dune, the desert fell away into a deep valley. The sand brushed lazily across a stone path that wound it's way northward, towards cooler climates, and more hospitable countries. Rumbling along this road, a small caravan of carts meandered. They moved with the laziness of repetition. A wandering motion that eluded to the regularity of their surroundings. Rajhu knew the look well. He had needed to master it, in every country, in every city... With *it*, he could blend in, be accepted, and gain people's confidences. From there, he could often gain their gold.

'Hey!' Will called, waving his hands above his head. 'Over here! Hey!'

Rajhu looked wearily to the younger boy. 'Maybe they have water?'

'And maybe they're going the same way we are!' Will agreed. He slapped Rajhu on the arm, and started his descent of the dune, each leg moving the sand in bursts as he ran. Rajhu admired his energy, but decided it was best for him to not copy it. If he did, he was confident he would do little more than end up face down in the sand.

As Will approached the caravan, it slowed to a stop, many people exiting the carriages and greeting him. By the time Rajhu reached the group, they let out a great cheer, patting him on the back and extending welcomes in many different languages. He smiled at them as they ushered him, and Will, into the largest of the carriages. Inside, there were cushions and silks draping almost every inch of the place. A large hookah sat in the centre of the floor.

The Wishcharmer Saga: Beginnings

The traders urged Rajhu and Will to sit.

'They seem friendly...' Rajhu remarked, slumping down on a large red pillow.

'They're traders, travelling between Durjen and Akaron,' Will laughed. 'They're going exactly where we need to... Isn't that great?'

Rajhu nodded, forcing a smile as they were brought water. 'It's very nice...' He drank deeply, but pulled his bag closer to himself as the traders settled in around them.

'What's the matter?' Will asked.

'Just a feeling...' Rajhu shrugged. 'But... Keep your guard up.'

The carriage shuddered and began to move. Rajhu yawned in the cool confines. These traders were very happy to see them. Such an attitude was rare... He should know...

Rajhu... was a master... at making people... feel safe...

Darkness enveloped Rajhu. His mind simply went blank. He could feel himself falling into sleep, but couldn't understand why. Even in his exhaustion, he hadn't been ready to rest. Not with the traders eyeing him and Will in such a way: Not as a Samrian viewed someone in need of service. Not as a friend observed a friend... but as a banker observed a coin... Or a law-maker observed some new power...

His eyes snapped open, his body going rigid. Raj looked around at the darkened carriage.

How long had he been asleep?

They were no longer moving, and he could hear hushed discussion all around him. Looking to his left, toward the entrance to the carriage, he could see two men. They were thickly built, and had cloth wrapped about their faces.

Rajhu cursed silently.

These were not traders. These were Akrian Pirates! Men of the sand, pillagers. Murderers... Riders of the Worms, and commanders of the Kilrot.

Everything made sense now. He hadn't simply fallen asleep... They must have put something in the water...

He cursed again, this time aloud. He realised his mistake when the two large pirates looked to him, their eyes shining in the dim light.

One said something to the other in Akrian, while the other stepped forward, rising to his full height.

'Two people, walking in desert... I didn't think this be worth the time it takes...' he admitted. His voice was hoarse, stilted, and breaking out in a rough accent. He chuckled. 'Never upset to be proved wrong... What should I find in your bag, but *two thousand* flanks!'

'Appuja, look!' the other pirate called.

Rajhu winced as the pirate turned, his eyes falling, as Rajhu's did, on the solid gold lamp.

'Hah!' the pirate exclaimed. 'I have half mind to not cut your throats... simply for amusement, and gladness you bring me!'

He spun to face Rajhu again. He couldn't see the man's mouth, but felt him smile, nonetheless. 'But more of mind agrees that cutting your throat... please me as much as gold!'

He stepped forward, his hand moving to his waist. There was the unmistakable ring of steel, then Rajhu's eyes caught the glinting dagger. The man was closing in on him, and yet, he could think of nothing to do. The carriage was confined, and Rajhu was sitting. There was no time to think, there was less time to act.

The pirate lunged and Rajhu flinched, but the bite of the blade never reached him. As the pirate moved, Will sprang from across the carriage, colliding heavily with the man, and pushing him into the wall. Wood gave way under the assault, and the two tumbled away, into the evening light.

Rajhu scrambled to his feet as the second pirate moved away from the bag, dropping the lamp. He was nearly to the entrance before Rajhu met him. Ducking low, he rammed his shoulder into the pirate's stomach. The man groaned and fell backward. Raj snapped an elbow into the side of the pirate's head, feeling him go limp against the attack.

Turning in a rush, Rajhu grabbed the bag with his lamp and his flanks, and jumped out of the carriage. His feet hit the rough ground, skidding a little as he took in his surroundings.

Gone was the yellow sand and scorching heat of

The Wishcharmer Saga: Beginnings

the desert. Now, under his feet, coarse red shale stretched out in every direction. Large flat stones peeked out here and there, while hearty green shrubberies nearly three meters tall grew in the distance.

To his right, Rajhu saw Will rising from his clash with the pirate leader. Will held his arm tightly, crimson blood leaking slowly through his fingers. Rajhu gave the boy a smile and started toward him. Will stumbled, but took a step. Behind him, Rajhu could now see the form of the pirate Appuja, sprawled on the shale ground. He stirred as Rajhu closed in on Will. Then with a mighty scream, he slammed his fist onto the ground.

'Kilrot! I call thee!'

Rajhu froze.

Will looked to him in terror. He knew the stories of the Akrian pirates, as well as Rajhu did. He knew the tales of the monstrous worms they rode, and of the dreaded Kilrot, a beast from the depths of the sand.

Rajhu had no idea if they were too far north, now,

but the ground was still soft, and the earth behind them shifted.

Suddenly, a form burst through the shale ground, a scream ripping through the warm evening light.

Rajhu saw the form rise up behind Will. It was big, and at least a dozen tentacles dragged it forward. At the end of these, a large pod-like mouth slithered on the ground, its round form giving way to a beak filled with needle point teeth.

Tentacles snapped forward, wrapping around Will's legs and pulling him roughly to the ground. The beast screamed again as it dragged Will backward, towards its open mouth.

Rajhu dropped his bag, a scream clawing its way free from the depths of his person. He rushed forward, not knowing what he could do. He was just a man, and had no hope in a battle against a Kilrot. Still, he wouldn't leave Will to this. Not after everything they had been through together.

Gold light screamed free from somewhere, and Rajhu turned to see it. It snaked its way from his bag, weaving through the air before colliding with his chest. In that moment, every nerve in his body suddenly came alive. He gasped as the surge fell over him. He didn't understand, and yet, something in the back of his mind was awakening. Something ancient alighted through those nerves. Something powerful.

Raj turned on the spot. He leapt forward, crossing the distance between himself and Will in a single, massive bound. His arms reached out, almost of their own accord, grabbing hold of one of the slimy tentacles. It writhed under his grip, but Rajhu paid it no heed. Something was pushing him through this encounter. He didn't know how he was to achieve victory, only that he would.

The Kilrot pulled against him, but Rajhu held strong. His arms locked, his muscles tensed. Even so, as it was, he couldn't reach the head of the beast, and therefore, couldn't engage it in any kind of battle. This was one of the great defences of the Kilrot. Before you could attack, it already had you.

Even as the worry washed over him, Rajhu felt something stirring within. A power he couldn't explain raged at the thought of Will's demise. That power cycled back on itself, growing ever stronger. With a mighty roar, Rajhu felt something happen.

Two great pillars of blue light burst from his shoulders. The energy swirled about, and the pillars formed into giant arms. He looked on in awe, but a calm settled on his mind almost immediately.

This was his weapon.

Rajhu tightened his grip on the tentacle, while the arms of energy, or magic (he wasn't sure), stretched forward. Chorded with muscle, and slightly transparent, the arms reached out, grabbing the Kilrot's mouth. Rajhu slammed the beast's head against the ground, then hit it, hard, with a giant fist. The Kilrot screamed, and as it did, he thrust the hands back, grabbing at its beak, and tearing it open. The beast screamed again, but the snapping of its jaw cut the cry short. The beast fell limp against the ground, its tentacles losing all their strength.

Will stumbled free, gasping.

The arms vanished from reality as Rajhu turned.

Pirates were encircling them from every side, swords drawn. Their eyes darted between Rajhu and

The Wishcharmer Saga: Beginnings

the dead Kilrot.

Rajhu set his stance, thrusting his arms forward. As soon as he had, another wave of blue burst from his body, forming, as before, into blue arms and hands. He swept the pirates away, throwing them into the air. They screamed as they tumbled. Their cries were muffled as they collided with the ground.

Rajhu turned to the carriage, the blue hands wrapping around it. With a strain of effort, he lifted his hands, the blue counterparts following the action. Rajhu thrust his hands outward, and the carriage was thrown high. It hung in the air for a moment, before descending in a rush, crashing into pieces as it hit the ground.

Pirates were returning to their feet now, but as Raj turned to face them, they ran in the other direction, screaming in Akrian, words Rajhu couldn't understand.

Will looked at him, as the mystical hands evaporated once more. Rajhu stumbled back, his eyes wide.

'What... What just happened?' he asked.

Will shook his head. '...I, ah...'

'Am I a magician?'

'Let's just... get out of here...' Will insisted.

All around them pirates scattered, and before long they were disappearing into the distance. Rajhu stumbled to his bag. He paused for a moment, looking at the lamp that sat near the top.

'What is it?' Will asked.

Rajhu grabbed up the lamp, then slung his bag over his shoulder. 'I don't know, Will... But I need answers...'

Will nodded. 'We'll find them, then. Come on, Cavrey is just over the horizon. I heard the pirates talking. If we hurry, we can make it there before the sun completely sets.'

Rajhu looked up. To the west, the shale ground rose into a distant, rocky crag. The sun was slowly lowering itself behind the tall hill. Finally, he nodded.

'Alright... Let's get out of here, before I do something else impossible...'

Will smirked. 'You mean like play hero twice in one day?'

The Wishcharmer Saga: Beginnings

Raj smiled, but said nothing. He shifted the bag on his shoulder, setting himself to the problem at hand. It wasn't far now, to Cavrey. Once there, he would start on it. Something had happened to him, and Rajhu was set on making it right.

Vance Smith

The Wishcharmer Saga: Beginnings

6

The Kilrot stank of death.

As Gwendolyn approached it, there were still coyotes feasting on its flesh. She marched ahead of the procession. Breaking from the ranks of soldiers, she walked toward the carcass of the desert beast. Beside her, Babo walked lazily.

'It's jaw has been snapped...' she observed.

Babo nodded. 'Wishcharmer...' he hissed.

'If all you've told me is true, then... How has he

displayed this level of power so suddenly? He was created not two days ago, the Djinn claim.'

The cat nodded. 'Two days... No more. This kill is fresh. Happened... last night, maybe. He isn't far, now, Gwendolyn. We should keep moving...'

Nodding, Gwen turned from the corpse, striding back to the large group of soldiers. All eyes fell on her. All eyes locked on her garb. Gwen was dressed in the sacred armour of the Sorceress. It was a symbol of her power, of her position. She could glean the fear in the eyes of the soldiers. Sorcerers, whoever they were, demanded respect, for fear of their power. It did not matter what kingdom or city one was from, fear of the Sorcerers was apparent everywhere. It was this fear that allowed Gwen to do her job.

'I want one hundred men stationed here, day and night, until I return. Blocks three and four, that's you! The rest of you, accompany me. We're heading to Cavrey.'

'Do you honestly believe three hundred soldiers is enough to contain a Wishcharmer?' Babo asked, coming to stand beside Gwen.

The Wishcharmer Saga: Beginnings

'I've no idea what the appropriate response is, Babo. This isn't something I'm familiar with.'

'That much is obvious, Gwendolyn... But who among us knows what to do in these circumstances?'

'These are soldiers of Geb. They're given the same training as the Sorcerers personal guards...'

'Don't fool yourself, my dear. They're nothing of the same kind. The Guardsmen are honed by magic. Crafted into weapons. These men are not much more than arrow fodder. Bravery is their greatest resource.'

'Something I hold in great esteem.'

'As you should... But do not be lulled into believing it outdistances power, by its sacred nature. Even the divine God above does not protect men from their own stupidity.'

'Then we had best make sure we make no stupid moves.'

Gwen thought she saw Babo smile, but she was never sure with the creature. After another silence, he nodded. 'By your grace, Sorceress...'

The soldiers shifted as Gwen gave the command. One hundred of her men began setting up camp in the decimation left by this Wishcharmer. She would have them guard it until her return. There was a chance this Wishcharmer was still nearby. She would risk the journey to Cavrey, though. It made the most sense. Either way, she would glean something from this mess. There was some clue, hiding either in Cavrey, or here. It would point the way for her. It would lead her to this Wishcharmer, and she would stop him. If she didn't, as Babo had explained, a war would break out. One that the Sorcerers themselves feared to fight. With such a foe, she would not rest until he was subdued. This, she swore.

The Wishcharmer Saga: Beginnings

Vance Smith

3rd

Passage

The Magi's

Revenge

7

Cavrey's green hills and lazy rivers washed the heat of the desert away in a matter of hours. The small country was home to a circular mountain chain called the Pearl. The white, snowcapped peaks shone out for all to see, and marked the unavoidable turning point to the world. They were moving north, and things were cooling down.

Rajhu smiled to himself as he and Will made their way down the well trod road. Grass stood defiantly against the dark earth. While put underfoot by many people, the little shoots still climbed skyward. It was the optimism of nature. Rajhu respected it, and felt something similar stirring within himself. Things had taken a turn for the worst, but he could now see the hope in all of it. That hope was centred in the city of Dwel.

'Come on, Will... Nearly there now! Dwel we go, and we rid ourselves of this curse!'

'Your curse, Raj. Not mine,' Will smirked. 'Honestly, I don't know why you're so set on getting rid of this magic, anyway. You saw how handy it was against those pirates!'

'I'm not a magic kind of guy, Will. I know, all you young people like to talk about the days of Sorcerer wars and Djinn armies, but I don't think like that. I'm a simple man. I have *simple* needs.'

'Gold?'

Rajhu smirked, shaking a finger. 'Lots of gold, my friend. Lots of gold!'

Will rolled his eyes but said nothing as he and Rajhu moved down the lane towards the white walled city of Dwel. Traffic picked up considerably as they

The Wishcharmer Saga: Beginnings

neared. Carriages and travellers of every conceivable creed bustled about the entrance.

As he crossed through the gateway, Rajhu looked up at the massive white stone that made up the walls of Dwel. It was said that in times of war, those walls could withstand any attack. Kings had boasted that not even a sorcerer could break them down. Rajhu considered it a blessing on those kings that they had never needed to put their boasts to the test.

Moving through the crowds, Rajhu led the way deeper into the city. The sun was well into the sky, and though there was heat to the day, it was far less oppressive than the desert. It was closer to his homeland, and the temperate climate made him feel at ease.

'Where exactly are you leading us? I mean, I don't have all day to be wandering around...'

'Nonsense, Will. We're fugitives with a fortune in our bags. We don't have anything to do *but* wander!' He paused. 'Besides, before we do anything else... I want to rid myself of this magic. I have an old friend here in Dwel. He'll set us on the right path. Before the spring is out, I'll be my old charming self once again!'

The city was circular in nature, with countless cross sections and winding paths cutting through the otherwise round roads. Rajhu knew the streets well, but hadn't been to Dwel in some time. Though he wasn't as confident as he would have liked, it wasn't long before he recognised several landmarks.

They hurried through the streets, the crowds growing denser as they neared the castle, which towered over the city. Placed on a tall hill, the castle truly was the marvel of Dwel. As the city walls boasted impenetrable strength, the castle stood as a lone bastion against the harsh realms that surrounded it. The seat of power stood out amongst warring factions as the strength of reason. At least, that's what Rajhu's friends insisted on telling him.

All he saw was another monument to nothingness.

'Here,' Rajhu croaked, turning down another backstreet. There were no people here, and a pungent odour swelled from the dimness. Two tall housing complexes rose four stories on either side of them, blocking out most of the sun. At the end of the short street, a building cut off escape, ending in a battered wooden door. A sign was hung lazily above the door, though Rajhu couldn't read the script, he knew what it said. This was home to Garrot Weed.

'It says this is a magic broker, Rajhu...'

'Garrot deals in anything he can gain from.'

'And magic is one of those things?'

Rajhu shrugged. 'On occasion, I have been told.'

He didn't need to look. He could feel Will tensing behind him.

'I'm as willing to go into shady places as you, Raj... But something feels funny. You sure you want to go through with this?'

'Infinitely.'

Rajhu lead the way into the cramped building. The smell of incense hung heavily in the air. Squinting against the dim light, he stumbled forward.

'...Anybody home?' Will asked, stopping just behind him.

'Nobody you'd like to meet, boy...' a voice croaked out.

Vance Smith

Rajhu peered into the depths of the room as a form trundled forward, stepping close to them, but staying well back from the light cast from the open door.

'Raj... It's been a while. You didn't bring guards with you, I assume.' The man's voice was harsh and low. Rajhu couldn't be sure if he'd only just woken up, or perhaps the man was a little angrier than usual. Either way, it was of little import. Rajhu wanted answers, and he would have them.

Slipping the bag from his shoulder, he let it hit the ground, kicking up dust in the process. Hastily, Rajhu undid the drawstring and removed the lamp from it's home, then held it out.

'Tell me what this is... Go on. Give me an answer, Garrot. Tell me exactly what I've done, and how to get out of it...'

Silence pressed on the room as Raj held the lamp steady. Garrot, still veiled in shadow, shifted on his feet, drawing a tattered robe tighter about his thin frame. Slowly, he took a step forward, his ragged face entering the edge of the light. Deep, fresh scars

The Wishcharmer Saga: Beginnings

wound their way from his forehead to the lowest part of his chin. Rajhu tensed as he took in the shape of the man.

'Time... hasn't been good to you, my friend...'

'The world has changed, Rajhu...' Garrot hissed, grabbing the lamp and stepping further into the light of the day.

Will edged away from the man, giving Rajhu an uneasy glance.

'Maybe the world has changed... but...' he hesitated. 'Who gave you those scars?'

Garrot had his back to Rajhu, but slowly looked over his shoulder, a smile crawling into a sneer. 'Djinn...'

Will took a step back. 'The Djinn did this to you?'

Garrot shook his head. 'No, boy... Soldiers did this. Dwel has taken a harsher stance against the underworld, as of late. I've become a statistic of their handiwork.' He threw the lamp back to Rajhu, who only just managed to catch it.

'The lamp... *That's* Djinn. That's what I was trying to tell you. That there... It's a Djinn lamp, Raj.'

'I don't understand...' Rajhu whispered. 'I didn't wish for magic. I didn't wish for help... Why then... Why am I cursed?'

Garrot scowled, moving back into the darkness. 'What's he yammering on about?'

'Rajhu has magic. He destroyed a caravan of pirates, just outside the city. He thinks he's been cursed or something.' Will explained, folding his arms across his chest and leaning in the doorway.

Garrot turned suddenly. Even in the darkness, Rajhu could see the man's eyes blazing. Was it fury, or fear that consumed the man?

'Where exactly did you *acquire* that lamp, Rajhu?'

Raj shifted, stuffing the lamp back in the bag, and hoisting it onto his shoulder. 'Doesn't really matter... I just wanted to know if the lamp was connected...'

Garrot shook his head. 'You *meddle*, Rajhu! You always meddle! Don't you understand that there are powers beyond reason in our world?' He walked up to Raj, his eyes wild. The man grabbed hold of his shoulders, shaking him. 'If you took that lamp from a Djinn... If you *split* his magic...' He shook his head,

The Wishcharmer Saga: Beginnings

but released Raj, stepping back into the shadows.

'Garrot... I need your help!' Raj insisted.

'Go from here! Tell no one I spoke to you! ...I want no part of it, Raj! I want no part!' he hurried away, into the depths of the building. A door closed in the distance, and silence enveloped them.

Vance Smith

8

Cavrey's cool air put the mood of the soldiers at ease. Gwen wasn't sure if she liked the idea of it, really. The last thing she needed was for her men to be taken off guard now, when they were so close.

The Wishcharmer was here, in this very city. Babo had confirmed it, though Gwen herself was still unsure how.

'You're unsure of how to proceed?' the cat-like creature asked from near Gwen's feet. She bristled, looking down with a scowl.

'I'm perfectly capable of completing the mission, Babo. There is a reason Salvidi trusted me to this.'

'And there is a reason he invited me to come along, as well. Please don't be combative, Gwendolyn. I am but a servant of the cause. We are on the same side.'

Gwen sniffed, looking across the city as they marched on. Trees grew in manicured lines throughout the streets, hugging the curved roads and caressing the sides of the taller buildings. In the air, birds chirped in the morning light. They were still a day behind this Wishcharmer, and though it was still early in the morning, Gwen was on edge. They needed to find him. She hoped Babo was right. She hoped they had arrived in time.

'Do you know of any way we can locate this Wishcharmer?' she asked, looking to the cat.

Babo tittered. 'We will be made aware of his location.'

'We will?' She smirked. 'And do you mind telling me how this will be done?'

Sighing, the cat stopped, forcing the column of soldiers to do the same, just behind him. He shook

The Wishcharmer Saga: Beginnings

his head and looked up at Gwen. 'Perhaps Salvidi should have told you more... Never mind, I suppose....' He nodded, before continuing. 'The Wishcharmer is wild, and has no idea how to control his powers, yet the vengeful Djinn has not been contained by their council. This was done in good faith.'

Gwen furrowed her brow. 'I don't understand. I always thought the different councils didn't care for each other.'

'They do not have any *direct* animosity toward one another. However, you are correct in your assumption. There is no *official* distaste between the ruling councils of the Djinn, Sorcerers and Goulems... However, time has given way to... diverse disagreements.'

'They hate each other silently.'

Babo nodded and started forward once more. 'Very astute. In regards to the appearance of a Wishcharmer, however... They have managed to put aside their various differences.'

'So they let this angry Djinn wander around... I

don't understand how it is supposed to be a boon for us.'

'This is the very same Djinn who was wronged by our wayward Wishcharmer. While I'm not permitted to discuss details, I will tell you that the Djinn is partly responsible for the creation of the Wishcharmer, but because of this, he has lost nearly half of all the magic power he possessed.'

'Half Djinn? Then it's a Magi...'

'A very vengeful Magi, my dear. One who pins the blame of his lost power squarely on the shoulders of the man we seek.'

Gwen scoffed as they moved deeper into the quiet streets of Cavrey. It was a bold plan, but there was no guarantee it would work.

'My scouts have seen the Magi wandering the edges of Cavrey. Undoubtedly, he has found our Wishcharmer for us.'

'So we wait for him to pounce on the prey?'

'Precisely. With any luck, we will be able to subdue them both with relative ease.'

'But... He will be out for blood! I thought we were

meant to bring this Wishcharmer back to Geb alive!'

'That would be the ideal outcome. We must discover exactly how he came to be. If for no other reason, then to assure it never happens again.'

Gwen sighed. 'I still don't understand why these Wishcharmers are so dangerous!'

'The answer is simple, my dear Gwen... The Wishcharmers threw the universe into chaos eons ago. They are the sole cause of the misery of war. The archetypes of destruction. They were the enemy in the last great war of the universe.'

Gwen felt something catch in her chest. The burning heat of fear washing over her as Babo's words wound their way through her mind. She had read the sacred books. She had learned of all the wars, but none had been more terrifying to her than the last great war. The war to end all wars, it had been called. The three great powers of the universe, locked in immortal combat.

She had read of their foe. A force more powerful than any that had ever been known. Their name had been whispered on the wind for as long as she had sensed it's passing. The horde of darkness. The Star-Killers.

'Sufficed to say, we have little time to waste,' Babo insisted, hurrying forward. Gwen nodded, though she knew the cat hadn't seen it. He was concerned with the task at hand, while she still couldn't comprehend what she had learned. If it were true, if this Wishcharmer was one and the same as the Star-Killers spoken of in the Holy Books... Their world, and every other life in creation, across the oceans of heaven, was in danger.

9

Rajhu wandered out of the inn, letting the cool summer breeze wash over him as he took in the sights of the city. It had been many a year since he had wandered this close to his homeland. Even now, with it countless leagues away, it felt close.

Still, ever since he had been confronted with this curse, this magic power that seemed to be ebbing and flowing just beneath the surface of his conscious mind, Rajhu hadn't had a moment's peace. He couldn't have kept the fact that he was shaken from

Will. Least of all, he couldn't have hidden his terror at the reaction of Garrot. Whatever had gone amiss in Durjen, had done more than Rajhu had ever feared it could. Things were out of his control, and it seemed as though they would never be made to yield to his will again.

'Maybe we should just move on, now...'

Rajhu turned to see Will walking up behind him. He had Rajhu's bag slung over his shoulder. A worried look flickered through the boy's eyes, though Rajhu pretended not to notice it. Will wasn't one to let people see his concern. The fact that it was showing spoke to Rajhu of the situation he had put them in.

'Eeh...' he shrugged. 'I don't know what to do now, Will. It's all gone bad.'

'So... Let's just get out of here. There's nothing left to see anyway.'

'You've seen all Cavrey has to offer in a day?' Rajhu asked, smirking.

'We spent the night in a dingy inn,' he shrugged. 'I can get that anywhere I go.'

The Wishcharmer Saga: Beginnings

'I still haven't figured out what's wrong with me, Will!' Rajhu relented, frustration flashing through him in a rush. 'I want to be normal again! I don't like all this magic, you know. Never cared for any of it. Life is life, and I just want to get on with living it...'

Will shrugged. 'I gotta tell you, Rajhu, I think you're making a big mistake.'

'What do you mean?'

He shifted, moving the bag from his shoulder, and setting it on the ground in front of him. 'Well... Maybe what happened isn't as bad as you're making it out to be...'

'Oh, come on, Will! Giant blue hands came out of my back! That's not being normal, man!'

Will smiled. 'No... No, it's not normal... But it's pretty cool, too...'

Rajhu canted his head, narrowing his eyes in observation of his friend. Had everyone gone mad but him?

'Look... You've been given incredible powers, Raj. I mean, you don't even know what you can do, do you? This could be good for us, you know. And who knows? This might be *fate.*'

'I'm fated to be cursed?'

'Don't think of it like a curse, Raj... Maybe you're *supposed* to have this magic, this... power.'

Rajhu paused. He hadn't thought of it like *that*. In fact, if he were honest, he hadn't given any of this much thought since it had happened. Garrot's reaction had scared him, but the fact was, he had been faced with a horde of Akrian Pirates, and came away with barely a scratch. Against a dreaded Kilrot, Rajhu had been victorious.

'You're actually considering it now, aren't you?'

Rajhu waved off Will's comment with a flip of his hand. 'Shush. Let me think about this for a moment, okay? There is a lot to consider...'

A gentle breeze ruffled Rajhu's clothes, whispering through the manicured trees that hugged the side of the inn. The warm summer air seemed to calm him all the more, and yet, he still could not decide what he thought about all of this. Magic had been given to him, but at a cost he couldn't quantify. What had he become? Was it something good, or something very

The Wishcharmer Saga: Beginnings

much the opposite?

'You took something from me, Rajhu Heroh...'

The voice cracked through the air, as if it were the sole sound in all the world. As it fell into silence, Raj could feel every nerve in his body coming alive. His skin tingled with terror as a figure walked up the street. Raj stared at the sight of the man. Dressed in dark, loose clothing, the man was large, with golden skin, and a trimmed white beard.

'Do I know you?' Rajhu asked hesitantly.

The man inclined his head, then swept his arms about his body. 'I admit, my appearance has changed since last we met, but I am one and the same. You took something from me, Rajhu Heroh... I would very much like it back...'

There was no doubt of it in Raj's mind now. Though he had changed, though his body was chorded with lean muscle now, the eyes held the same dark glint.

'Raj... Who is this?' Will asked, stepping closer. Raj could see the boy tensing, readying himself for a fight. He had no idea what good it would do, though.

83

'My lamp... Raj. *My* lamp!' The man growled. 'I want it back!'

Taking a step back, Rajhu looked the man over once more. To him, here and now, he looked like a man, and nothing more. Could it be true that this elder was actually a Djinn?

It didn't take long for the man to reach Rajhu. He grimaced as he reached out with strong hands, grabbing Raj's collar. 'If you won't give it to me, I will *take* it from you!' he spat.

The man lurched to one side, tossing Rajhu away with incredible strength. He tumbled through the air for but a moment before crashing to the hard ground. He rolled to a stop, groaning as scrapes and knocks of pain flashed across his person. Rajhu struggled, but pushed himself up off the ground. He was a good four meters away from the old man now. As he looked across the distance, he saw Will striding forward, shouting at the man. Rajhu wanted to call out to him, to tell him to stop, but everything was happening so fast.

The man's hand struck out, catching Will in the

The Wishcharmer Saga: Beginnings

side of the head, sending him tumbling through the air. He collided with a nearby fruit stand, and slumped to the ground.

Rajhu forced himself to his feet, his head spinning. As he worked to steady his footing, the man moved across the street to Rajhu's bag, ripping it open.

'Hey!' Rajhu called, stumbling forward. 'You can't just do such a thing!'

The man straightened, pulling free the glittering form of the lamp. He flicked his free hand, snapping his fingers. Instantly, a burst of flame sailed forth, exploding at Rajhu's feet.

'You dare object to this?' the man growled. 'After you take my property from me, after you defile this sacred vessel! I am Ferro, Once Djinn over the Eastern Sea... Made Magi, by *your* violation!'

'I *paid* you!' Rajhu countered. 'It's all a legal transaction!'

'I should tear out your tongue for speaking to me in such a manner! Do you not know who you've crossed? You and your little friend here have taken the lamp of a Djinn!'

The man rushed forward with inhuman speed. Before Raj could react, a hand was firmly clamped around his throat. Rajhu tried to breath in, but it was impossible. This Ferro was far too strong - Beyond anything a human should have claim on.

'Take...' Raj gasped. 'Lamp...'

Ferro tossed Raj to the ground. He lifted the lamp in one hand, looking down on Raj with wild eyes. 'Unfortunately it's not that simple, Rajhu Heroh. I've already tried to bond with my lamp with no success... You have taken something from me that cannot be returned...'

Rajhu tried to stand, but a scowl from Ferro told him it would be better if he stayed on the ground. Still, he forced himself up onto an elbow, rubbing at his throat tenderly.

'I give it back to you, freely. Whatever it is I took, I give it back. Just leave us in peace!'

'Leave you in *peace?*'

'Let us be!' Rajhu insisted.

'You still have no idea what you've done, do you?'

Rajhu shook his head. 'I've wronged you... I am

The Wishcharmer Saga: Beginnings

sorry. But please, I... I want no trouble. Take what you've lost, and go... Please!'

'My dear boy...' Ferro laughed. He stepped forward, a hand reaching down. Rajhu felt himself hauled to his feet, his attention drawn to the rage of the Magi's eyes. 'You've harmed me... In a way I cannot express to you. Even my harshest punishment wouldn't suffice to show you the pain you've caused...'

Ferro flicked his wrist, and again, Raj went flying through the air. He didn't know where he was tumbling to, until his back collided with the stone wall of the inn. Something cracked under the assault, though Rajhu was sure it wasn't his bones.

Pain snapped through him as he fell to the ground. When he finally looked up, the Magi was there, the lamp grasped in his hands, his eyes seeming to flash red as he glowered down on him.

'You've split my magic... Broken an ancient seal. You may have harmed me, most foul... But you've done worse to yourself, yet!' He crouched down, a fist hammering into Rajhu's face. Darkness crept at the edges of his vision, but he pushed back against it. He wished it back with all his might.

Slowly, his vision cleared.

The fist came again, and Rajhu lifted a hand, but before he could block it, a wave of blue energy washed in front of him, taking the brunt of the impact. The shimmering magic hung in the air before his eyes, like a bubble.

Ferro laughed, pulling his hand back. 'And there... you see? It's already begun...'

Rajhu glanced from his hand to Ferro, something stirring inside. 'What's begun? Do you... know what's happening to me?'

'You've cursed yourself, Rajhu Heroh... you've split my magic, and awakened a dark power within yourself...'

'What do you mean?'

'You've become a Wishcharmer... Rajhu. It would be in my best interest to kill you, right now...' He lifted his hand again, rolling his thumb across the tips of his fingers. As he did, electricity crackled into life. Soon, its form grew, curving into the unsteady visage of a scimitar. The Magi stood, a smile curving across his lips.

'Goodbye, Rajhu... Know your death will bring me a moment's purest pleasure!'

The electric blade plunged downward, and Raj held his breath, bracing for the end, when a voice cut through the street, loud, clear, and angry.

'Hold, I say! By the authority of the Sorcerer Council, and in directive action for the Djinn Hierarchy! Desist!'

Raj waited a moment, but when no horrible pain pierced his chest, he cracked his eyes open, looking in the direction of the voice. As he let his eyes open wider, they beheld a young girl, dressed in polished leather armour. She had long black hair that hung, braided, to the base of her back. Strong, dark eyes held him and the Magi like a vice. Her soft features, while fair, were cold as she observed the scene. A large cat sat at her feet, its tail coiled around itself. Behind the two of them, a very large number of armoured soldiers stood. In a great ringing of steel, they drew their swords, taking one step forward, past the girl.

Vance Smith

Raj glanced to the Magi, then gasped. The blade of the conjured scimitar hung only inches from his chest, but Ferro was not paying any attention to him, at the moment. His dark eyes bore through the empty street, lingering on the young girl.

'What say you, girl? Do you think I care what authority you claim hold on? I am Magi! I fall under no direct council! The Djinn do not want me, and your pathetic Sorcerers... Hah! They would as soon kill me as this beast that lays before me!'

'Ferro... You don't want this fight.'

'You are right, girl. I have no wish to engage you. Perhaps you would let me do what I came here to do, and then you would owe *me* a favour!'

The girl's voice came again, a grumbling edge to it now. 'You know I can't let you kill him, Ferro.'

The Magi chuckled, furrowing his brow. 'And why should I suppose to know any such thing? He is a *Wishcharmer!* By the very dictate of every council you have claimed privy power from, he is sentenced to death, by very fact of existence! Tell me I'm wrong, and I will lay down my sword... Otherwise, let me finish this, and have my revenge!'

'The council's have dictated that the Wishcharmer be kept alive... for now.'

Rajhu couldn't believe what he was hearing. Whatever this Wishcharmer business was, these two people seemed to think he was one. Whatever a Wishcharmer was, he was certain he didn't want to be thought of as one, considering the callous nature in which the Magi and this girl could discuss his eminent, or eventual, demise.

'Don't I have a say in this?' Rajhu asked.

'Quiet, whelp! Lest I slit your throat before hearing the young Sorceress out...'

There was a silence from the ranks of soldiers. In another moment, the girl pushed her way through the line of men, planting her feet and staring at the Magi.

'I propose a trade...'

Ferro smiled. 'But you have nothing to offer me, child. I am a wanted man, ever despised by the Djinn for this revenge I sought. A fallen Djinn, and you speak of a trade... Trade of what, dear girl? Stories?

You have nothing I want, and I have everything you desire.'

'We won't take you, if you hand us the Wishcharmer... *Alive!*'

'My freedom?' Ferro laughed. 'Young Sorceress, I hope you haven't yet studied the arts of negotiation. Elsewise, your instructors have sorely done you a disservice. I have my freedom!' he insisted, throwing his arms up. 'You cannot bargain with it, when you haven't the power to take it from me.'

'I will, if I have to...' the Sorceress growled.

'And I will kill the Wishcharmer before you raise one hand to strike me,' Ferro countered, smiling as he returned the point of his blade to Rajhu's chest.

Things were spiralling out of control. If he didn't do something quickly, he would be dead. If he waited for these two to settle things, they would end up fighting each other, which would likely mean he would be dead.

He hated the Powers... They never let anything remain simplistic.

While the Magi and the Sorceress continued to

The Wishcharmer Saga: Beginnings

throw threats at each other, Rajhu desperately tried to think. There had to be some way out of this! Some kind of escape he hadn't thought of already...

For a moment, Rajhu wished he'd had powers, magic... Like the kind he'd used in the desert, against the Kilrot...

Magic...

Rajhu cursed himself under his breath. Of course! He *had* power! He *had* magic! While these two argued over it, Rajhu remembered with alarm, just the kind of magic he had.

Was this what all the fuss was over? This magic he had used... This was what a Wishcharmer was?

It was the escape he wanted, and needed. But how could he use this magic? How had he done it in the desert? Thinking back, he realised he hadn't really thought on it all that hard... It had simply been reflex.

'Reflex...' Rajhu whispered.

'Shall I cut out your tongue to keep you silent?' Ferro barked, turning to stare down at him.

Rajhu smiled. 'You forget, my boy... You're dealing with a Wishcharmer!'

He threw his hands forward, willing the magic forth, from whatever ancient well it sprung from. He envisioned huge ethereal hands launching forward, and blasting the Magi across the street.

As it was, nothing at all happened.

Ferro looked down on him with increasing disgust.

With a glance to the Sorceress, the Magi scowled. 'Do what you will, young one. For now, I shan't stand in the presence of this abomination a moment more. Now he dies, by my hands!'

Rajhu cursed under his breath.

'I *really* wish that had worked...'

The Magi thrust the scimitar towards Rajhu's heart, but as the magic blade drew near, blue energy burst free from his palms. The smoke-like magic swirled and formed into huge fists. They rushed forward, throwing the Magi across the street, and through the stone wall of the adjacent building.

'Stop him, now!' the young Sorceress cried, but Rajhu was already climbing to his feet and dashing across the street.

Rajhu bent low, scooping up Will in one arm, as

he threw the other skyward. More of the blue magic streamed forward, as soldiers, rushed them. Rajhu suddenly felt the magic that wound it's way across the sky connect with something. Looking up, he could only just make out the giant blue hand, as it seemed to grab onto thin air. With another thought, Rajhu felt himself pulled from the ground in a rush of speed. The magic was drawing him up, and forward, over the city, toward the sky, as it wound itself up, like a fishing line being drawn back, in a rush.

Below him, Rajhu saw the Sorceress and the soldiers looking on helplessly, as he shot higher and further away from them. They grew smaller as they receded into the distance. Looking about, Rajhu could see he was sailing high above the countryside, the walls of Cavrey nearly an hour's distance away already. The lush green meadows of Cavrey's farmlands fell away rapidly into thick forest and rolling, steep hillsides.

Suddenly, the magic flickered, then faded away altogether.

Rajhu hung in the air for a moment, Will's

unconscious form held firmly with one arm.

'*Koliba!*' he cursed. They slowly began to plunge toward the earth. Fear clawed at Rajhu's mind, as he shifted in the air, trying to position himself better, for what little good it would do... Below them, a forested hillside sped up to meet them.

Rajhu felt himself impacting the hard ground. He felt trees shattering around him, he felt rocks digging their way into his skin. Then, he didn't feel anything.

Then... everything went dark.

The Wishcharmer Saga: Beginnings

Vance Smith

4th

Passage

Buri's Retirement

Home for Ageing

Warriors

10

Birds chirped from somewhere above. There was a buzzing, but it wasn't clear where it was coming from. As Rajhu's eyes slowly fluttered open, bright light suffused his vision. He tried to move, but thought better of it when pain the likes of which he had never known spiked through his body. Groaning, he resigned himself to shifting slightly instead.

What had happened? Why was he so broken down? And why was everything moving past him, if he was lying still? The world rattled, and he rolled over, looking ahead of himself. As he did, the unwelcome sight of a horse's backside came into view.

He clicked his tongue. 'This is what I wake up to, now?'

Beside him, Rajhu could hear Will stirring. He rolled again, taking a look at his young friend, who lay beside him, bandages wrapping his shoulder and left arm.

'You two boys are mighty lucky to be alive, you know...'

A hand settled on his shoulder and Raj saw a man walking beside the cart. He had a thick frame, and though he was an elder, his aged body was still corded with muscle. Grey eyes observed Rajhu from a weather-lined face. The man scratched at a brushing of white stubble on his strong chin and smiled. 'But perhaps... it's less luck than I thought...'

Raj knit his brow together, struggling up into a seated position. 'Who are you, uncle?'

'Me?' the man laughed. 'I'm Buri.'

Rajhu started, giving the man a second look. He was old. Perhaps in his seventieth year. Though age was relative, Rajhu wasn't able to reconcile the age of this man with his name.

'B- Buri?' He questioned. Not taking his eyes off the man, Rajhu groped around with his free hand, slapping at Will. He heard his friend wince, cursing lightly under his breath.

'Raj... I swear, I'm going to gut you! I-' Will scrambled up, pulling his fist back as he struck out for Rajhu.

'Will, look, it's Buri!' Rajhu barked.

Will faltered, stumbling onto Rajhu as he stared at the old man walking beside the creaking cart.

'B-Buri?' Will stuttered.

Rajhu tilted his head. 'That's what *I* said...'

Will crawled over Rajhu, sending a knee into his stomach. Raj groaned, pushing Will forward, almost sending him tumbling out of the cart.

'Buri, like... I mean, as in Fredrik Dorzen Buri?'

The old man smiled, giving Will the smallest nod. 'Yes. Though... I haven't heard my whole name since I was in swaddling.'

Will laughed, throwing a hand back and slapping

Vance Smith

Rajhu in the chest.

'Raj, it's Buri! You know, the greatest swordsman to ever have lived? He's *that* Buri!'

Rajhu wheezed as he repositioned himself. 'I thought you'd be pleased...'

The old man raised an eyebrow. 'You're not a swordsman, are you my boy?'

'Who, me?' Will laughed. 'Ah, no... I don't know. I wouldn't call myself a *swordsman*. I dabble...'

'Dabble...' The man smirked. 'Son, we *all* dabble. It's a hell of a lot easier to say that, than to announce to the whole world your craft. If you only dabble, well... You don't get into as much trouble, do you?'

'You would be surprised at how much trouble he gets into, sir Buri...' Rajhu insisted.

Will gave him a look, and Rajhu rolled his eyes. It was to be like this, he supposed. Will had talked of this Buri many times over the years. As he'd said, it was widely accepted that he was the greatest swordsman to ever have lived - a claim that had caused the man countless battles, and countless riches as he was sought by kingdoms to fight in their

102

The Wishcharmer Saga: Beginnings

wars and tournaments. That didn't even begin to delve into the kind of gold the man made in training...

Will cleared his throat. 'What are you doing in these parts? I mean, the last anyone heard of you... It was thirty years ago, and you were near the sea of Constantine. Most everyone thinks you're dead, sir...'

'Oh, please...' the man scoffed. 'Me? Sir? No, no... That won't do at all. My name's Buri. It was given to me for a reason. People might as well call me by it.'

Will giggled. Rajhu glared at the boy, which did no more than cause him to repeat the action.

'What are you doing, Will?'

'I'm sorry, Raj. But I mean, the greatest swordsman who ever lived or fought just asked me to call him by his name.'

'Don't mind the boy, sir Buri. He's a little dazzled by you.'

'Hmm, so it seems...'

'My name is Rajhu... The giggling boy is Will. We're simple travellers... Down on our luck.'

Buri nodded. 'Now *that* I can understand. But never fear. All travellers are welcome here. And any

103

boy who *dabbles* in swordsmanship is a friend of mine...'

Will's smile grew past what Rajhu thought was physically proper, and again, he giggled.

Rajhu sighed, letting his eyes droop. He supposed such was the way of young people. They were easily influenced by the sight of their heroes. Even Rajhu had to admit some excitement at being in the presence of a legend. There was a thing called decorum, however. He didn't see why Will was incapable of exercising a little of it at the moment.

'You boys have a reason for being this far up the mountainside?' Buri asked, a knowing twinkle gleaming through his glance.

'We...'

'Yeah. Raj... How did we get up here? The last thing I remember is that Djinn coming at me...'

'Djinn?'

Rajhu waved Wills comment aside with a flippant gesture as he smiled at Buri. It took a good deal of his remaining energy to conjure up the expression. Even so, he was confident it held little substance. 'It turned out it was a Magi, honestly. No big thing, I assure you.'

'Uh-huh...' the old man nodded, the twinkle returning to his eyes. 'And yet, I found the two of you at the base of a crater. If I were a younger man, susceptible to fantastic ideas, I'd have bet you fell from the sky, crushing that gouge into the stone.' He paused, raising a hand in a placating gesture. 'Ah... If I where a younger man, you understand...'

Rajhu held his smile, letting his head bobble side to side. 'Sir Buri. We... don't want any trouble. It... simply has a way of finding us.'

'Say no more, Rajhu... I may be on in years, but I can still figure out a thing or two on my own. Don't take this the wrong way, but... I think I have you all figured out.'

The cart began to slow as it crested a rise on the winding stone path. As it clamoured over the last peak, a wide meadow opened up before them. Rajhu could see birds in flight as they darted from one tree to the next. Forest teemed at the edge of the meadow, with soaring evergreens, and wide poplars. Short grass lay underfoot like a rich carpet laid by the creator of the universe. Across the way, sitting just in front of the beginning of the forest, stood a large log home of four storeys. It was an elegant affair, but rooted in the work of a man's hands, making it retain a humility not afforded to the mansions of the great cities.

'Sir Buri... What is this place?'

'This? This is my home, Rajhu. Welcome to Buri's Retirement Home for Ageing Warriors...'

Buri stepped forward, slipping his hand into the halter of the horse, leading it gently across the meadow, toward the building. Rajhu stood up in the cart, steadying himself against the uneven ride. He shifted his feet, and looked over the horse at the approaching building. There was a small porch covered by an overhanging. There were chairs set out, and even from where he was, Rajhu could see a pair of elders seated on the porch, talking. They turned, waving to Buri as the cart came to a stop just short of the porch.

'A couple of new arrivals, Buri? Look a little young

The Wishcharmer Saga: Beginnings

to my eyes,' a wrinkled man with a skiff of white hair atop his head said, laughing.

'I don't think they're here to stay, Xur. I found them in a crater down on the lower slopes.

'Xur?' Will laughed. 'Xur Keffet? The man who took two thousand men against an army of ten thousand, and didn't lose a single man?'

Xur laughed, running a hand over the little hair he had left. 'It was a long time ago, my boy. No need to dwell on it...'

'No need?' Will scoffed. 'Sir, you're a legend!'

'We're all legends here, Will.' Buri smiled, walking up onto the porch and leading Rajhu and Will inside. 'Of course, at this point in our lives, we just want to be left alone. Maybe have a game or two now and then.'

As Will and Rajhu entered the building, they saw dozens of people, ranging in age, wandering about a wide room. There was a bar to one side, and smoke hung heavily in the air. The acidic smell of it mixed with alcohol and drifted to Rajhu, its sharpness stopping him in his tracks.

'You all live here?' he asked.

Buri nodded. 'There's a passel of rooms upstairs, and a couple more buildings this size, just back a ways, into the trees.'

'Why?' Will wondered. 'I mean, you could go anywhere, do anything!'

'When you're my age, my boy, you don't want to. No, what we have here is perfect. We have our freedom, and our lives. That is more than any warrior dares hope for.'

'But the mountains?' Will protested. 'I mean, you people deserve better...'

'We deserve whatever we build for ourselves, Will. With our own hands... No one owes us anything, and we claim no privilege, save the right to be left alone and to live as we please.'

Buri led the two to an open lounging area. There were dozens of soft chairs laid out, with short bookshelves sitting beside them. About half of these chairs were occupied by people. Rajhu recognised a few of them, though they looked much older than any portrait he had ever seen of them.

The Wishcharmer Saga: Beginnings

They passed a woman who must have been in her late years, past eighty, Rajhu would have guessed. Her hair was snow white, bushy, short, and curled tightly. She fingered a diamond pendant around her neck. The jewel was as clear as water, save a small ruby coloured stone at its centre.

'Is... Is that Madame Resolux?' he asked, stepping to Buri's side and leaning toward him conspiratorially.

Buri laughed. 'Yes... Although, don't... don't mention that business with the Djinn war in the north...'

'You mean when she battled with four giants? How she bested them, *and* managed to steal a horde of treasure they had kept in their mountain cave?'

Buri nodded, leading them to three empty seats that faced a large window. It looked out the back of the building, a trail snaking across its view, then slipping into the extensive forest as it climbed up the side of the mountain.

'Sit, please...' he smiled, sinking into one of the ample chairs. 'You know, I was amazed when I came upon you, Rajhu. Such a thing, I haven't seen in many, many years. Do you mind telling me how you survived such an impact?'

'Me?' Rajhu questioned, stiffening. He had no idea what to say. He was wary of telling anyone what had happened to him, considering the reactions he had received from friend and foe alike. This Wishcharmer business was far beyond him, and the longer he remained in this state, the more he feared he was becoming some kind of monster.

Rajhu shrugged, smiling candidly. 'You never know what the Divinity has in store for you, correct? I suppose, it was luck...'

Buri laughed resting the side of his head on his hand, and considering Raj. 'That's quite a thing to say, isn't it?'

'What do you mean?' Will asked, sitting in the seat closest to Buri. Raj continued to stand. He felt himself growing more and more anxious. With this man's questioning, he wasn't sure if it would be a good idea to stay here very long.

'Well, your friend here invokes the Divinity as cause for his survival, and in the same breath, credits

The Wishcharmer Saga: Beginnings

luck as the reason he stands alive, after crashing into the side of a mountain...'

'I wouldn't say I crashed,' Rajhu laughed. 'Such things... They are impossible, no?'

Buri smirked. 'No, Rajhu. You don't get to fool me. You see, I witnessed your arrival on my mountain. I saw with my own eyes as you slammed through the stone flesh... You are a wonder the world has not seen in quite some time.' He laughed, leaning back in his chair, letting his hands fall onto the armrests. 'Yes, I haven't seen strength like that since... since...' He looked past Rajhu, his eyes unfocused.

'Since what, Buri?' Will asked.

Buri took a deep breath, his smile returning. 'Wishcharmer... You're a Wishcharmer, aren't you?'

'I... We're just travellers, Buri...' Rajhu stuttered.

'Wishcharmer?' Will asked, furrowing his brow.

Buri nodded. 'Yes, it couldn't be anything else, could it?'

'No!' Rajhu snapped. 'I'm not a monster!'

'Rajhu, Wishcharmers aren't monsters...' Buri attested. 'They're powerful... feared. But there are very few things in this world that are inherently evil. Wishcharmers, are not one of them. Although I'll admit, I haven't seen a new Wishcharmer since the great purge in the east...'

'What are you talking about?' Will scoffed. 'I've never heard of any Wishcharmers before...'

'There are more of them?' Rajhu asked.

'Oh, a few... Not many. Perhaps... twelve, not counting you. The purges took the lives of most of them. You see, Wishcharmers are one of the great Universal Powers. The unfortunate thing is, the other three fear them, as if they were a plague. The only Wishcharmer I've seen in over fifty years would be... Rua. Rua Fíoch. He's the only survivor of the last purge. Of course, that wasn't many years ago. I believe, if I remember correctly, the Djinn eradicated his tribe. Slaughtered them to the last man. But the last man escaped. Rua's not been the same since. I've tried to tell him, show him the writings. There are a few more Wishcharmers out there. A few left alive... But he was destroyed by the purge. His spirit was crushed.' Buri smiled sadly. 'Rua used to be such a happy boy...'

Rajhu shook his head. This was all too much to process. He couldn't take all of this in, not at once, not like this...

'What if I... don't want to be a Wishcharmer?'

'There's little that can be done about that, Rajhu. You can run from your fear... but you can't run from yourself. Where ever you run, you will be there. But, as you said... the Divinity has plans, correct?' He stood, smiling at Rajhu. 'I would suggest... you meet Rua. There are few people who could help you better than he. You seem confused... Rua can explain things that I can't...'

'Could you take me to him?' Rajhu asked. He wasn't sure how to feel about any of this. He was still scared. He still feared that despite what Buri said, he was turning into a demon of some kind. But if there were another Wishcharmer, then maybe he could get to the bottom of all this nonsense.

'To Rua?' Buri laughed. 'He lives high up the mountain. In a cave he carved with his own hands. At least, that's the story he tells me. Yes, I can take you to him... Just let me grab a few things. I'll take you now.'

Buri stood, walking away from them. Will smiled as he climbed to his feet, stepping up to stand by Rajhu.

'See... Didn't I tell you everything would work out? We'll go talk to this Wishcharmer, and he'll explain everything. You'll see.'

Rajhu had no idea what to believe anymore. He forced a smile, and nodded, however. 'I am sure you are right, Will.' He bobbled his head, 'Let's just try and keep our wits about us, okay?'

Will gave him a lazy smile, 'Whatever you say, Raj...'

There was a great commotion near the entrance to the building, drawing Rajhu and Will's attention away from their predicament.

There was a sudden bout of shouting, and Rajhu turned more directly to face the entrance. He could see many of the elderly inhabitants standing up and peering through the windows that hugged either side of the large wooden door.

The Wishcharmer Saga: Beginnings

'Buri!' a voice growled from beyond the barrier. 'Come out, Buri, or I swear I will come in!'

Will started toward the entrance, but Rajhu grabbed him by the arm. 'What do you think you're doing?'

'I'm gonna go see what's going on,' he explained, his brow furrowed.

'We are not owing these people anything, Will. Let's just keep our heads down, hmm?'

'Raj...' Will breathed, a look of displeasure crossing his face. 'We're already involved. And I'm not going to stand by and let something bad happen to these people. They're heroes.'

He pulled his arm free as the door to the building burst from its iron hinges and crashed to the floor. Will bounded up the steps and walked toward the door.

'Shaed...' Rajhu cursed. 'You're going to get us killed, Will...' He ran a hand heavily through his hair, then followed his friend.

Buri hurried from somewhere deeper in the building, striding past Will as a large man stepped through the entrance of the building. Rajhu cursed again as he saw the huge man run his deep brown eyes over the inhabitants of the retirement home.

Corded with thick muscles, the man stood taller than any of the people in the room. He had short, dark hair and a strong, sharp jaw. A scowl hung from his lips as he took another step into the building. The man wore a heavy suit of armour that covered him completely, save his head. The dark, unpolished steel looked matte in the daylight, and seemed to reflect not the faintest image. The whole body of armour was a terrifying plate-mail suit. To Rajhu's eyes, however, it looked more akin to great steel scales, as if the man who stood before them were some dragon, taken human form.

The skiff of a beard he wore hung only from his chin, and was, as his hair, trimmed short.

'Buri...' the man sounded, his voice a low, smooth tone.

'General,' Buri nodded. 'What is it that brings you here?' His voice was tight, though Rajhu sensed no fear in it. There was something else there. It wasn't anger. In truth, Rajhu thought it sounded more like sorrow than anything else.

'Give me the sword, old man...'

'Is that why you've come here, Val'kez? My answer is the same as it's always been. I will not hand over the Taintless Blade to the likes of you!'

'I will have the Blade, Buri. Despite what you think of me, I've done only good for this land. Now, when I attempt to continue this work, when I try to make peace in the world, you deny me the tool that would allow such work to take place.'

'You've no right to that sword, General. What you would do with it, the way you would use it, would be in violation with it's truest intent. I will not give you the Taintless Blade. Not today, not ever.'

The man took a step back, an armoured hand flexing as he looked over the gathered crowd.

'This man you hold in such esteem... Is an enemy of justice!' he growled. 'While the world out there rots... While the Powers conspire against humanity, he sits! You are as guilty as he is!' he spat. 'Whatever end comes to this world, the blood of every child rests on you! The screams of the innocent will haunt your ears, not mine!' He stepped to Buri again, his form looming over the older man.

'If you will not give me the Taintless Blade, after all I've done... Then I will take it!'

'Val... Think this through,' Buri pleaded. 'Don't force violence.'

'The blame is on your head, Buri. If the sword is not brought to me by moonset, I will return with my army, and you will know the full extent of my strength. I will burn this forest to the ground. I will end every last one of you. Then, I will take the sword from amongst the ashes...'

The man turned, storming out of the building, and out of sight.

Buri sighed, turning. His eyes searched for a while, before finding Rajhu's.

Raj could see a great sadness within the man, and though he wanted to turn from him, he couldn't.

'And now, you see... This is why I brought you here... I need your help, Rajhu. I need the majesty of a Wishcharmer. Only that can save us.'

The Wishcharmer Saga: Beginnings

Rajhu swallowed, his eyes never leaving Buri's. 'I am... at your service. Whatever it takes...'

Vance Smith

11

Moss clung stubbornly to the crumbling stone. Heedless of the cold air, or the pouring rain, it clung to the ancient castle. In the cracks that had resulted from age and war, the moss thrived. General Val'kez looked down on the soft, green growth. Despite everything, that moss had grown on the stone, high in the mountains. Like it, Val'kez had needed to thrive where others would die. In this, he had succeeded. There was far more to do, however.

Turning from the open window, Val put the moss

and the midnight storm from his mind. In the cold, small room before him, five of his commanders stood, huddled near the struggling fire they'd built in a small hearth.

'For generations, the destiny of humanity has been chained by the three Powers of the Universe. While they stand removed from our struggle, they yet refuse us the freedom to expand our strength. They lock away the beings who bore this world through the darkness at the beginning of time... They proclaim to us what we are to do. If only Buri knew what I've discovered... If he could simply speak to the force we intend to set free...' He shook his head.

'What do you plan on doing, General Val'kez?' a stout man asked. He was bald, and his face held little intelligence, but for Val, such a thing wasn't needed from the man. He was a brute. Val'kez was content to let the man live as one. Such a man served him well, and would, in what was to come.

'I will take the Taintless Blade from Buri. Nothing has changed, Deret.'

'But, General... Master Buri was-'

The Wishcharmer Saga: Beginnings

'I don't care for what he was!' Val'kez growled, taking a step toward the man. Deret shrunk against his advance, sinking into the group of men. He looked away, pretending to tend to the small fire.

'Even so,' Galak, Val'kez's second in command, grumbled. 'They do pose a threat... None of us possess the power that you do, General. Unlike you, we bleed. We are at risk.'

'We will not engage them, unless it becomes unavoidable. I will engage who I must. For you, it will be to keep anyone from escaping. The Taintless Blade will make me unstoppable. I must have it. If we are to bring war against the Djinn, the Sorcerers and the Goluems... I will need it.'

'Our army isn't assembled, yet. If we take losses before we reach Dwell, we might be routed.'

Val'kez shook his head. 'No. We are protected. The old god has told me.'

'Does his influence reach so far?' Galak asked.

'He is bound, but he still speaks to me. Our armies will be more than enough to deal with the Dwel guardsmen.'

Vance Smith

'Then why bother with this sword?'

'If we are to free this god, Galak... we must have blood drawn by the Taintless Blade. One way or another, we must gain this, before moving on... Before reaching Akri.'

'All this magic... I don't like it, General. Your armour is one thing... but my skin sets to crawling with this talk of dark oaths...'

Val'kez glared at the man. He flexed one of his armoured hands. 'With time, Galak... you will see. Everything I do, every sacrifice I make... In time, it will all be worth it.'

Galak bowed at the neck. 'Of course, General...'

Val turned back to the window, looking into the raging storm. He took a slow breath. 'Ready the men,' he growled, striding to the window. 'And bring me my sword. We march in an hour... At dawn, Buri will fall...'

Galak bowed again. 'By your command, General.' He turned, striding from the room.

'All of you... Get out!' Val'kez hissed.

He heard the rest scatter. He heard the whispered

fear. He knew all of it. What he planned to do terrified them. As it well should. By any means, Val would free this wretched world from the slavery it was bound to.

The Powers... They would fall. If Buri was a casualty of this war, so be it. They had both made their choices. Val'kez had heard the old one speak. Buri had not. No matter what happened, no matter what he did, Val'kez had to obey the old god.

There was no other way.

12

Dawn was breaking. The world outside was wet from the night's storm. The air was as fresh as any Will had ever known. It was a beautiful day. And yet, he shivered in the early morning light.

'What's wrong, boy?' Buri asked, coming to stand beside Will.

Looking to the old man, Will smiled. 'I needed some air...'

Buri harrumphed. 'So, you wandered out of the house for air? Wasn't there a sufficient supply inside?'

The Wishcharmer Saga: Beginnings

'I...' Will tried, but Buri waved a hand.

'I'm only teasing, Will... I know what you're feeling.'

'You do?'

Buri nodded. 'You're scared. Terrified, if I'm correct.'

'I don't know if I'd go *that* far...'

'Aren't you?' The man asked, dipping his head, his strong eyes boring into Will.

'Yes, sir... I am.'

'A better response than I got from your friend...'

Will arched a brow. 'Raj? What did he do?'

Buri waved a hand again. 'He pretended to faint... It's reasonable, I assume. Neither of you want to be put in the middle of our little war, and yet... that's exactly what I've asked you to do...'

'It's not like we have a choice... I mean, even if we left, they'd probably send someone after us, too.'

'That's a tactical idea... I suppose they would. Send someone to make sure you don't have what he wants.'

Will nodded. 'I've heard about it... But I always sort of thought it was part of the legend, you know?

Master Buri, cutting through the side of a castle to take out a despot... I never really believed the Taintless Blade was *real*.'

Buri laughed, patting Will on the shoulder. 'If only it were a legend, Will...' He shook his head. 'Alas, things are never as easy as we wish them to be. Sometimes the Divinity puts things before us. Tools, which could as easily be used for evil as they are for good. I think He puts them before us as a test. To see what we do with such power.' He paused, taking a slow, even breath. 'I hope I've done well with the power I've wielded. But the time to use such power is past... At least, it is for me.'

Will furrowed his brow, looking to the man intently. 'You're going to give up your sword?'

'I can't see another course of action. Even with the help of your friend, Rajhu... We're too few in number. We need every warrior we can muster. Some of us are simply too old now, Will. As much as we did, as high as we rose...' he shook his head. 'Time takes its toll, you know...'

'But...' Will tried. 'Do you really think that guy will

use your sword for good?'

The man smiled, his eyes sad. 'No, Will... I suppose he won't.'

Looking up, Buri scanned the sparsely treed yard. The early morning light seemed to paint the short grass in shades of orange and pink. He stood for a long moment, silent.

'Would you accompany me somewhere, Will?'

'Sure, but... shouldn't we start making plans? General Val'kez will be here soon.'

'Yes... So, we will make plans. Come on, I have something I need to show you...'

The old man turned, hurrying toward the large building. Will followed as Buri climbed the steps of the porch and slipped into the building. The lounge on the main floor was empty now, as it had been most of the night. He lead his way through the room, trailing off to the right. Beside the bar, hidden by a wall, a small staircase climbed to the second floor in an unwavering line.

'What's this all about, Buri?' Will asked.

The man was silent as he climbed the stairs.

Reaching the second floor, he walked down the long hallway. Doors lined the walls, large silver numbers hanging from their faces. He stopped at the last door on their left. Will saw a tattered number clinging to the door, but it was in a strange script he'd never seen before.

'What's this?'

Buri opened the door, stepping in.

It wasn't a large room, but it was tidy in its layout, making it seem less crowded than it actually was. A large glass window was built into the roof, letting in the soft dawn light. Even so, it was enough to reveal the contents of the room, and in so doing, its purpose.

Every wall was lined with swords of every imaginable variety. Each weapon was placed and hung with intricate care. Hundreds of them hung against the four walls. Wooden displays dotted the floor as well, each full of swords.

In the corners of the room, large wooden barrels stood, stuffed full of even more of the masterful looking swords.

Will turned around several times, looking, but not

able to take in every one of the weapons. There were legends here. True legends.

'It's my collection. Some of these aren't mine, actually... I've bought a few, and more were given to me by swordsmen and women from my travels...'

Will found the capacity to nod, then turned again, his eyes falling on a glass cabinet in the centre of the room. Only one sword was within, and unlike most of the swords on display, this one was firmly rooted in its scabbard.

Buri walked to the glass, touching it softly. The surface shimmered and vanished in a barely audible rush. With two hands, he reached in and lifted the sword from its stand. He turned to Will, holding the weapon up.

'This is my prize... The sword that took me from a boy who *dabbled* in swordplay, to the man so many called the master...'

'The Taintless Blade...' Will whispered. 'So it *is* real...'

'Yes, Will. It is... And more than that, it's powerful. More so than you could possibly imagine... This sword is different. It's not a creation of man. And so, it's powers are greater than even I have been able to understand.'

'What do you mean?' Will asked.

'I mean, it's not just a sword... It's a warrior, a priest, and a vulture... This sword, alone... could defeat empires. I can't let it fall into the hands of a braggart. And yet, I'm constrained from using it anymore... I'm too old for this blade, Will... I don't want what it brings.'

Will eyed the man suspiciously. 'Then what do you plan on doing with it?'

Buri smiled. He looked down on the scabbard, running the back of a finger across its surface.

The sword looked heavy in his hands, but he held it deftly, as well he would, having wielded it for so many years... The scabbard was of polished blue, with silver strappings at the tip and the mouth. A strong cross-guard of polished steel stood out from the wrapped hilt. The pommel, too, was polished.

'The Taintless Blade had never indulged to telling me its own desires. At least, that's what I'd thought...

The Wishcharmer Saga: Beginnings

It has guided me through my travels, protected me from evil... and what it asked, I never understood.' He looked up. 'Though it spoke, though I heard, I never truly understood...'

'Buri, I don't have any idea what you're talking about...'

The man chuckled. 'I suppose you wouldn't... This sword isn't forged of man, but of Wishcharmers...'

'*What?*'

Buri nodded. 'It's true, Will... And there will be much more you learn about this forgotten group in the years to come... They are feared, above all else... They were the greatest of the Powers of the Universe. Even this sword, itself, is alive... When I asked it, time and time again, what I should do with it, when my fighting days were done, it always answered the same. "Give me unto thy own will..."' He laughed, 'I never understood... But I do now...'

Gripping the hilt tighter, Buri drew back, pulling the blade free from the scabbard. A loud sound rung out as it was released, like glass scratching stone.

In a flourish, a perfectly clear blade was drawn out

from the scabbard. Buri stepped to Will, laying the blade in his hands, as it shimmered in the low light, catching the sun. The sword was larger than Will had imagined, but none of that compared to the impossibility of the blade.

'It... It's...'

'Diamond,' Buri finished. 'And forged, too... Look, the fuller is of the finest workmanship...'

Will had to agree with the man. A finer sword, he had never seen. And yet, the whole thing was made from a material he'd thought impossible to forge.

Will stared down at the blade for a moment longer, then pushed it toward Buri. The man stepped back, shying away from Will and the sword.

'What are you doing?'

'It's you, Will. You're the one the Taintless Blade has chosen. As I wielded it, now you must, too.'

'Buri, I... I'm no master swordsman,' Will insisted. 'I wouldn't know the first thing about how to use such a... such a powerful weapon. I'm *not* the right person for you to pass this to.' He shoved the hilt into Buri's hands and stepped back, wiping his hands on his pant-legs.

'You *are*, Will. I've watched you from the time you arrived...'

'Which was *yesterday!*'

'...You have a different way about you.'

'You *can't* know that! Buri... You can't just expect to know the right person from seeing them...'

'I have been waiting for the next bearer of this sword for a very long time. I have known what that man would look like, what he would sound like, for a very long time, Will. Regardless of your faith in my judgement, I am correct in this. With all that you are going to face, with the trials that are ahead of you, the Taintless Blade is yours.'

'What trials?'

Buri shook his head. 'Will, you are the companion of a Wishcharmer. Do you know what that means? Every country, every soldier, every Power of the Universe will seek you out. They will hound you for one purpose... To kill you.'

'What?' Will snapped. '*I'm* not a Wishcharmer!'

'It doesn't matter if you are or not. You're his

friend! The Wishcharmers are seen as a curse, as destroyers of stars, of worlds! They are spoken of as an unstoppable plague that will bring about the end of everything!'

Will stopped, his heart hammering in his chest. The stories, the Magi, the way Rajhu's friend had reacted... It was all linked to this Wishcharmer business.

'Is it true?' Will asked, his voice no more than a whisper.

Buri was silent.

Will looked at the man, his eyes finding the master swordsman's. He shifted, avoiding Will's gaze. The simple reaction sent a cascade of terror through Will, making his skin crawl. It couldn't be true... Not all of it, not with Rajhu...

'Buri...' he said, his voice growing an edge. 'Is it true?'

The man looked up, the sword lowering in his hands.

'Will, there is much about the world that we can't understand... The Wishcharmers... They're-'

The Wishcharmer Saga: Beginnings

'Sir Buri! Sir Buri!'

There was a great commotion, drawing Will's attention. He turned as Buri looked up. Rajhu rushed through the open doorway, skidding to a stop before he collided with Will.

'Rajhu, you're awake...' He forced a smile. 'What can I do for you, my boy?'

Raj took a rattling breath, his eyes wide. 'They're here!'

Will felt his stomach lurch. 'Already?'

Rajhu nodded. 'Many soldiers...'

Buri growled under his breath, sliding the Taintless Blade back into its scabbard. 'Val'kez...' he breathed.

'What do we do?' Rajhu wondered.

Buri sighed, slowly looking to Will. He lifted the sword again, extending the hilt to him.

'We are warriors, Rajhu...' Buri frowned.

Will nodded. He saw himself reaching out, his hand grasping the hilt of the Taintless Blade. As his hand met the soft cloth wrapping, he felt something surge through him. He couldn't explain it, but it set afire every sense he had. He felt the purity of rage shift through his veins. The need to protect Rajhu, and the people of this little home arose in him like a storm. He pulled the sword from Buri's grasp and looked up, meeting Rajhu's eyes.

'Warriors fight.'

The words felt like thunder from his lips. They were not a platitude, but a commandment. A promise.

As he moved from the room, the sword firmly in his grip, Will knew, in his heart, that things had now changed, and would continue to do so, from this moment, and forever.

The Wishcharmer Saga: Beginnings

Vance Smith

5th

Passage

Restoration

of a

Wishcharmer

13

Ahorn sounded in the distance. Raj felt a shiver crawl up his spine at its call. Ahead of him, Will walked down the long hallway. While Rajhu felt an overwhelming panic taking hold of his mind, Will seemed collected. He couldn't understand why.

'Rajhu my boy, what have you gotten yourself into?' he breathed, hurrying to catch up to his friend.

As they descended the stairs, Rajhu could hear the commotion from the yard. Although he hadn't had much time to focus on it, he had seen the gathering force. He hadn't known how many soldiers there were, but it was more than he thought was reasonable. Even now, as they drew closer and closer to this seemingly unavoidable conflict, Rajhu felt his heart beating heavily in his chest. He wasn't a fighter. No, not in the least. Rajhu was a swindler. A con artist. There were few situations in which he was susceptible to violence. Even when such an occasion arose, his first instinct was always to run away from the battle. Here, now... Rajhu was walking headlong into it.

'Will... Wait just a moment!' Raj called, grabbing his friend by the arm.

In a flash, Will rounded on him, his eyes a storm of anger. 'What?'

'You understand you're marching into a war, Will?'

He paused, his eyes studying Rajhu for a moment. They flicked away. 'Raj... What else can we do?'

'Maybe there is another way... Maybe we don't have to blindly deliver ourselves to death's cold hands!'

Will scoffed. 'I don't have any plans to die, Raj.'

The Wishcharmer Saga: Beginnings

'Then *why* are we involved?'

'Because that's what we *agreed* to do, Raj!'

He rolled his eyes, putting his hands firmly on his hips as he looked away. Rajhu sensed Will had no less fear surging through his own veins, but beyond this, the drive to help these people, to stop this slaughter, seemed to be greater.

Rajhu turned to face Will, but before he could utter a word, Buri called out to them, hurrying toward them. Glancing to the entrance, Raj could hear the mulling of the crowd outside. Even from his limited vantage point, he saw the great numbers that had come to this place.

'Will, the blade...' Buri insisted, coming to stop between him and Rajhu. 'You hold it now, but I warn you, it is a great responsibility... Every warrior who has used it has been tested by it. Take care to bridle your passions, or they will destroy you.'

'What are you talking about?' Rajhu demanded. 'What blade?'

Will shifted his weight as Rajhu looked to the sword held at his side. It was secured in a heavy looking scabbard, but from all the talk he had heard over the years, he knew what that sword was.

'Rajhu... It's not as bad as you think,' Will placated.

'That sword is a legend, Will!'

Will paused. 'Wait... you're *okay* with this?'

Rajhu tilted his head, 'Can it help us survive?'

Will looked to Buri, who nodded in turn. 'It can lead you to victory, and more... As long as you take control! Will, I can't stress the fact enough. The Taintless Blade is as alive as you or me. It doesn't take kindly to upstarts, either. Control your feelings, master yourself, and you will master the Taintless Blade!'

'I don't understand...' Will admitted.

'Very soon, you will...'

Rajhu looked from the old man, to the gathering army outside the building. He felt himself wilt at the man's words. There had been a great part of him that had been hoping for something a little more substantial. Something that would drive him and Will to face this challenge.

'What about me?' Raj asked, after a silence.

The Wishcharmer Saga: Beginnings

Buri canted his head to the side. 'What of you, Rajhu?'

He stared at the man. 'What about me? You said you needed the majesty of a Wishcharmer to win this battle. You said that I was a Wishcharmer...' He clicked his tongue in distaste, looking away. 'You made me feel important...'

Buri chuckled lightly. 'Oh, Rajhu... You are needed. More that I could possibly explain to you. You are a Wishcharmer... And Will wields the *sword* of a Wishcharmer. Together, I believe, you can bring that majesty to pass. *Together,* as it has always been, yes?'

Rajhu looked to the man, the words piercing him. It had, as he'd said, always been the two of them. Rajhu and Will. So long now, it had been their friendship that had brought them through the hard times. Rajhu dared not think of the days before he'd found Will. As he looked once more, to the men outside, as their enemy screamed from beyond, demanding surrender, demanding this *Taintless Blade*... Rajhu nodded once more. Despite his best intentions, and despite all his instincts screaming for him to run, to hide, he still nodded.

'Together, then... Into the fray...'

Will smirked, the two walking side by side to the doorway.

14

The sun was higher now. The sky held streaks of pale blues and fading pinks. In the distance, Will saw the dark forms of storm clouds retreating. Fleeing from the carnage that they knew was about to unfold on the earth below them.

'Who are you?'

The voice clawed Will's attention to the source of the words. He looked down, to the hulking figure that stood only a few paces away. His hard eyes observed Will with disgust, his strong, jagged features speaking only of a power that Will dared not deny.

The armour covered his body, feet to shoulders. Only his head was exposed. The dark steel, like his features, was hard, jagged, menacing. Each piece of the intricate design seemed to roll back on itself, leaving not one break, not one weakness. It was methodical in its structure, and mechanical in its appearance.

'General Val'kez,' Will said, his voice shaking. 'I am Will...' he faltered. He had no surname. Like Rajhu, he was an orphan, yet he knew nothing of his parents, beyond where they had lived. He had no name to call his own. Besides Rajhu, all he could call his own was his freedom.

He lifted his head a little higher. 'I am Will Freeman; master of the Taintless Blade.'

Beside him, Will could feel Rajhu wincing. A boast, Rajhu always said, was no more than an axe hanging over your neck, unless you were positive you could back it up.

'*Master?*' The General spat, looking Will over with his iron gaze. 'You are no more master than I am

The Wishcharmer Saga: Beginnings

slave, boy... Now hand over that sword, before I am forced to pry it from your dead corpse.'

Rajhu stepped forward, pointing at the General. 'A challenge!' he shouted.

A silence separated them for a moment, before the hulking form of armour turned, his eyes falling on Rajhu.

'What are you prattling on about?'

Rajhu took another step forward, reaching the very edge of the buildings deck. 'I issue a challenge to you, General Val'kez! You against us! If we win, you leave here... And if you win...'

'You die.' Val'kez growled.

'Then it is an agreement?' Rajhu asked, swallowing his fear. He stepped back, glancing to Will.

'The General grimaced. 'There is no deal... If you are the first who wish to die by my hands, then by all means, step forward... But know that I will not leave here without that which I came for... I swear this.'

Rajhu took in a sharp breath.

'If that's what you want...' Will growled, 'then come at me!' With the sound of glass scraping stone,

Vance Smith

Will drew free the glimmering form of the Taintless Blade. The diamond sword shone in the morning light. Will drew the sword down to his side, holding it lightly in his hand as he descended the steps of the porch to the soft grassy yard. Rajhu drew another deep breath and followed Will down.

General Val'kez cracked his neck, glancing behind him to the mass of soldiers. 'Got, Yemet... Take the shivering fool. Leave the *Freeman*, and the sword, to me.'

From the ranks of soldiers, Rajhu saw two massive men break free. They were clad in simple armour, each with a battle-axe hanging at his hip. They looked dirty, stained with mud from their travels. Their eyes were dark and empty, and as they charged, Rajhu cursed himself for ever leaving the city of sand.

Will leapt forward, colliding with the General. They tumbled back out of sight as the two burly men reached Rajhu. Axes in hand, they swung wildly, screams ripping through them as they hacked. Rajhu threw his arms out, unable to think of what to do. He ducked, a wish springing to his mind. A wish to survive.

How had he been so effective against the Magi, back in Dwel? He had stood against him, with great strength. If he were a Wishcharmer, as he'd been told, then how did it profit him anything, without knowing how to use such power?

He surged upward, magic bursting from his chest. Blue mist coiled, forming into arms, and grabbing the throats of the two attacking men. Rajhu let out a shout as he pushed forward with all his might. The ethereal arms acted as he commanded, bringing his attackers up off their feet, before plunging down, smashing them both into the ground. Air rushed from them as the power of the attack displaced in the ground around them, rupturing the surface of the soft earth.

As his foes lay motionless at his feet, Rajhu straightened, looking across the sea of warriors. Their faces contorted in confusion, fear, and rage. It didn't take long for several dozen men to break ranks, pulling free jagged weapons as they rushed at Rajhu.

He took in a sharp breath. 'Oh, Koliba...'

15

Will gasped as an uppercut crushed into his stomach. He retreated, falling back several paces as he desperately tried to regain his breath. This man, this General Val'kez was nothing short of a mountain, trying to crush him.

Will surged forward, bringing his sword up. He lunged, swinging the Taintless Blade low, going for the man's midsection. The attack found its mark, but cracked off the armour, without leaving so much as a scratch.

The Wishcharmer Saga: Beginnings

'How do you expect to beat him that way?' a voice scolded from Will's side. In front of him, the massive form of General Val'kez took a step forward, a smile crawling its way across his face.

'Stop looking at him, and look at me, Will... I asked you a question.'

Will turned, the image of Buri shimmering into existence before his eyes.

'You...' he tried.

'Quiet, Will. Your skills are hardly enough to carry you to victory against him... Not the way you're fighting, anyway... Oh, wait a moment... He's attacking. You should feint, then go for the neck. Feint now!'

Will stared at the man, then looked to General Val'kez, who was stepping forward, his fist swinging out.

'Oh, you should have listened to me...' Buri sighed.

Will felt pain explode against the side of his face, his jaw should have broken with the force of the attack, but it didn't. As he flew backward, crumpling to the ground, he could feel his face swelling as blood leaked free from his mouth. Will struggled to sit up, but fell back at the effort. His head rolled to one side, and as it did, the image of Buri appeared before him again, in an instant. It looked as though the air were piecing him together, like some impossibly complex puzzle.

'You're confused, right?' the man smiled. 'I don't blame you... But I do applaud you on containing your anger. It's a powerful emotion that could have easily destroyed you...'

'Buri...' Will slurred through broken, swollen lips.

The man shook his head. 'No... Well, I suppose you can call me that, if it makes you more comfortable. To be truthful, I'm more of a ghost... Well, sort of...'

Will groaned as he saw General Val'kez coming to stand over him.

'I'm actually a *copy* of Buri. Will, don't look at him. He won't attack you just yet.'

Will tried to scoff, but it was no use. He looked to Buri, his head swimming with pain, and now, confusion.

The Wishcharmer Saga: Beginnings

'Where was I? Oh, yes... I'm a *manifestation* of the man. You're right to suspect the sword... It made a copy of Buri, to store the sum of his knowledge. As it has done with every warrior who has ever swung this blade. I know it may be a lot to take in, but you should probably focus on this battle now... Oh, your friend is coming to save you. Look left...'

Will forced himself to turn away, slinging his head around. True enough, Rajhu was rushing toward him, blue mist stretching out from his chest toward General Val'kez. The mist congealed into fists, striking the General in the centre of the chest. Both men careened backward, out of sight. Will could hear the battle continuing as he tried to find the strength to stand.

'That's good, Will... That determination, that loyalty... The Taintless Blade likes you.'

Buri snapped into existence beside Will once more, a smile on his wrinkled face. 'You have a bright future ahead of you, but that's dependant on what happens here, today.' He sighed, glancing to the battle out of Will's sight. 'Now would be the

Vance Smith

opportune time to strike, by the way. General Val'kez is distracted, but he won't be for long... For a victory against such a skilled opponent, you're going to have to use surprise. I would say greater force, but you don't have it Will, not yet, anyway...'

Will glared at the man, who held up his hands in placation, then vanished. Silence enveloped him and he grabbed the hilt of the Taintless Blade harder than before. Buri hadn't warned him of this... He hadn't told him the sword would test him in *this* way...

Biting back a curse, he climbed to his feet, using the sword to support himself. He took a deep breath then, lifting the sword out of the ground, rushed into battle after Rajhu.

The Wishcharmer Saga: Beginnings

Vance Smith

16

Rajhu pushed harder as the General locked his feet, the armoured boots digging into the ground. Rajhu faltered as he saw the man smiling. He knew, just as this General Val'kez knew, the upper hand lay not with Rajhu, but with this warlord. He gritted his teeth, setting himself to the task. He had committed himself to this cause, however foolhardy that had been. He couldn't abandon it now, not even in the face of this monster of a man.

Goodness, what's become of me? My mind has

The Wishcharmer Saga: Beginnings

been poisoned by this blasted magic!

Val'kez grunted. 'You're a... *Wishcharmer?* That explains much of this. Why Buri would entrust the Taintless Blade to a child, and why he would hide inside his cabin, like a coward...' He shifted his arms, bringing them up, grabbing onto the undulating forms of Wishcharmer magic. The blue arms countered, trying to reach for his throat, but the General blocked them, with some effort.

'Do you even know how to control the power those ancients have given you?' He growled as he shifted the weight on his legs again. Rajhu felt the balance change. He tipped backward as Val'kez pressed his advantage. 'No... You have no idea. You disgrace the very idea of a Wishcharmer... For that, I will destroy you, and everyone who would stand with you!'

He shifted again, breaking through the lock that Rajhu had on him. Stumbling back, Raj gasped as the man collided with him. A series of punches snapped against his ribs, and before he could recover, he felt himself lifted from the ground.

The world spun in a flurry. Rajhu cried out as he

hit the ground, hard. He felt something in his arm give way, a wave of pain shooting through him. Looking up, he realised he was laying on his back. He tried to move his arm, but the effort was futile. With the pain of impact still coursing through him, Rajhu cursed as General Val'kez suddenly filled his vision.

'It doesn't matter. You may have the magic of a Wishcharmer, and your friend may wield a sword forged by the same power... But you still don't stand a chance against me, boy...'

'Then how about you take me on?'

Rajhu barely saw Will as he lunged at General Val'kez. He was moving faster than Raj had ever seen him move. It was an incredible display. He brought the diamond blade down, the heavy blow colliding with the General's armoured shoulder. Rajhu saw sparks fly from the impact as General Val'kez grimaced, stepping back, keeping his distance. He wasn't sure why, since the blow hadn't created any visible damage.

'You're still swinging that thing around like you know how to use it, *Freeman*?'

The Wishcharmer Saga: Beginnings

'I'll show you just how well I can,' Will growled. He stepped forward again, the sword coming up in a slash. Val'kez had to throw his hand up to deflect the blade, only just managing to keep the point from cutting into his throat.

The General spat on the ground, then looked to Will. 'I've wasted too much time letting you meddle in my affairs. You won't stop me. Not with that sword, or with that Wishcharmer pretender!' he pointed to Rajhu with a grimace. 'I will get what I've come for...' He glanced behind him, to the host of armour clad men and women.

Rajhu felt something inside of him sinking. Whatever was about to happen, he didn't like it.

'Kill them all!' General Val'kez roared.

The earth shook with the sound of cries and thundering feet. Rajhu could see the wall of death rolling toward them. The steel hearted horde was as merciless as it was numerous. This was beyond him, it was beyond Will...

Just in front of him, Rajhu heard Will growl. It was a guttural sound, and Rajhu could see the muscles tensing on his friend. Before he could call out to Will, before he could yell for his friend to run, to retreat, Will moved, striking out like lightning, the sword leaping in his hands.

The strike was exact, but even as it was made, General Val'kez was retreating. The tip of the blade slipped into his cheek, dipping into the flesh as easily as if it had been water. The man hissed as he stumbled, his armoured hand coming up to the deep gash, smearing the crimson across his gloved hand. He observed the blood, all attention to the battle drawn away by the insignificant wound.

As Rajhu watched, the General was engulfed by his army, the massive force flowing around him, obscuring him from view. The cacophony of enraged screams crashed against Rajhu as did the force of the enemy. For a moment, all he heard was noise. The bite of cold steel roused him from his confusion, but it was too little, too late. He pushed against one of the warriors, but felt a blade slip through his flesh, piercing his stomach. Rajhu moaned as the pain tore through him, only worsening as the knife was pulled free. He tasted copper in his mouth, and knew it wasn't a good sign. He threw his arms out, forcing all of his strength into the act. The magic forced its way out of his back, blue and coiling as it crashed down around him and Will, blasting many of the attackers off their feet, and throwing them back into their compatriots.

It wasn't much, Raj knew, but it had given them a little breathing space, and maybe, just maybe, a chance at escape.

Just removed from him, Raj could see Will straightening, that blasted sword held tightly in his hands. There was a bead of blood running into the fuller, painting the diamond red in its wake. Beyond him, the General held out his stained hand, a wilting frown solidifying on his face.

'For all your proposed skill, *Freeman,* you've not even delayed the inevitable...'

With a staccato shrug of his shoulders, Val'kez clenched his fists, his armour lurching. Two long blades extended from the elbows, running up along his triceps. 'In gratitude, I'll kill you painlessly.'

He jumped, launching far higher into the air than should have been possible. The armour fell in a heavy arc, the elbow-blade flashing as it reached for Will's throat.

Rajhu cried out a useless warning, unable to do more than watch.

Faster than Rajhu thought believable, the Taintless Blade came up, meeting the attack, pushing the vicious edges clear of doing unrepairable damage.

Val'kez kicked out, catching Will in the side and throwing him to the ground. Rajhu rushed forward, a tendril of blue magic snapping out and wrapping about Val'kez's throat. It constricted, but the General caught it, the elbow-blades coming up and cutting through it. Rajhu stumbled into the man, confused. How had he been able to break his magic?

A fist crashed into Rajhu's face, and he felt his jaw shatter as he crumpled beside Will.

This wasn't good. Not at all.

All around them, the army began to close in. They moved toward the house, their shouts and growls sounding, to Rajhu, more like a pack of wild beasts than humans.

Above him, above Will, the General glowered, watching as his army rushed around them, toward the log building.

'You're going to give that sword to me, Will. It's my destiny. All of this is unfolding exactly as the old one has foreseen. Now give me the blade.'

'I...can't-'

'Then die, and get out of my way.' The man stepped forward, his hands flexing before tightening into fists. Murder was in his eyes, and Rajhu felt not the least bit of strength in him to stand against it. Blood slipped from his mouth freely. The bone of his jaw had ripped through his skin when it had shattered, and even now, the pain was impossible to withstand. Now, looking up at Val'kez, Rajhu saw his death before him.

A scream rose up from somewhere behind Raj. From the ranks of the General's men, he could hear a battle taking place. He wondered for a moment if they had, at last, fallen upon the heroes of the retirement home, but when the body of an armoured bandit flew overhead, crashing into a pile of loose rocks, he wasn't so sure.

Looking up, Val'kez growled. He straightened as another mighty scream ripped through the crowd. Rajhu turned to see a dozen or more of the soldiers flying backward through the air. They collided with their comrades, taking even more to the ground.

Rajhu turned, looking in the direction of the commotion. He could see the host of soldiers beginning to turn, running in the opposite direction, back toward the trail that led down the mountain.

As the scene cleared, a man came into view. He couldn't have been many years older than Will, Rajhu was sure. He was short and thin, with lean muscle covering his body. A messy mop of red hair sat atop his head, sticking out in swaths of spiked and matted groupings. He had a soft face, almost boyish in nature, but a rage filled his eyes that was anything but. In his hands, the trunk of a splintered evergreen was held. The ancient trunk was far larger than he was, but as Rajhu watched, the boy swung it in a wide arc, batting away nearly twenty men as if they were flies.

The body of the tree cracked under the assault, and the boy threw it to the ground as he glared across the distance at General Val'kez.

'You want to fight, Val?' he screamed. 'You can't attack the old man's home and just expect to get away with it!'

'Rua...' The General growled.

'Come on, Val! If you think you can take me on, come here!'

The boy ripped the remnants of a shirt from his back, tossing the rag to the dirt. He shifted worn shoes into the ground, wiping his dirty hands on the stained, baggy white pants he wore.

'Men!' General Val'kez called, 'Move to retreat!'

'Not that easy!' Rua screamed, leaping forward. He bounded across the distance, landing before Val'kez, his eyes ablaze.

'You don't get to just run away! If you want to leave, let me show you the shortcut!' The boy screamed again, slamming a fist into the armoured stomach of the General. In a burst of dust and air,

Rajhu saw the General blasted back by the blow, flying high into the air, arching over the lawn, past the crest of the path that wound down the mountain, and out of sight.

'Anyone *else* wanna turn?' Rua growled, rounding on the remaining soldiers.

There was the slightest hesitation, before the mass of armour and weapons turned, scattering toward the path, screaming as they ran from the boy in the tattered clothes. As they fled, the noise went with them.

As silence slowly began to return to the large meadow, the boy turned, looking down on Will and Rajhu. The anger drained from him easily, a wide smile crossing his face. The expression only enhanced this Rua's boyish features.

With a young, high toned voice he gave a small laugh, 'bunch of wusses didn't even want to stand toe to toe!' He sighed, closing his eyes and smiling wider, still.

'It's kinda funny, I told Buri I only needed time to think about it... and he went and found a replacement for me...I guess the old man was right, though... It looks like I'm not the last Wishcharmer after all!'

Rajhu stared up at the boy as blood continued to slip from his mouth.

'Jeez, are you two alright?' Rua asked.

Vance Smith

End

Of

Beginnings

Stuff I say about people!

Thanks, of course go to God the Father and his Son Jesus Christ.

My family always supports me. It's like having an army behind you, with really cool gadgets and junk... but more of a family.

Cora has been a huge supporter of the Wishcharmer Saga. In fact, she likes it better than all of my other stories. That both hurts my pride, and excites me!

Patrick has created so many wonderful pieces of art for this adventure, and has been so gracious in helping me make this style of storytelling possible.

I couldn't have done it without these people, so give it up, raise the roof and do a dance! Hooray for these people I said stuff about!

The Wishcharmer Saga is an experiment in storytelling. I have been trying to create a world in which I can play, and nearly anything can happen. It has been a long road, and I've learned a lot. But there is so much more to come, and so much more to learn.

So ends Beginnings. When we next meet Rajhu and Will, there will be a celebration, but unfortunately... it's short lived. Thanks for giving the story a try. If you liked it, hang in there. Things are going to get really wild!

Until next time!

Oh, wait... there's more!

-Vance Smith, 2015

Vance Smith

Coda

Wayward Shadow

Vance Smith

17

The wind whipped across the desert, climbing the dunes easily, shifting them, moving them. While there was a lot of the wind that day, it offered no relief from the heat. Carrying sand in its heart, the gale assaulted Korel. Misery followed behind it, leaving nothing but the desire to be rid of this place.

He reached up, pulling the metal mask away from his mouth. It was a cumbersome thing, heavy, bulky. Two cylinders protruded from a smooth wedged plate that covered the mouth, allowing Korel to breathe,

The Wishcharmer Saga: Beginnings

even in the harshest of conditions.

He loosened the sand coloured cloth about his face, looking out to the twelve men that stood before him on the wasteland's shifting floor.

'You survived?' He asked, his voice hoarse.

One of the men, a large one with dark eyes, nodded. He was dressed in similar attire to Korel, albeit a crude imitation. Yellow cloth wrapped most of his body, to protect him from the storms, and hid him from investigating eyes.

Korel shifted the long, steel spear in his hands, ramming the butt of it into the ground. 'What do you have to offer me, Appuja? You left here with twenty of your best men, you left with a Kilrot beneath your feet. You swore to me an oath, in the name of the old god. You told me you would bring back what I sought, or die.'

Appuja shifted, his face twitching. Korel didn't know if it was from emotion, or simply cowardice. He didn't care.

'The man... The one you sent us for, he was powerful, Korel. He destroyed my caravan, he injured my men, slaughtered my Kilrot!'

'Did he kill your men?'

'No... But we were defeated. If we had pressed our attack, he would have-'

'Killed you,' Korel nodded, 'yes. So, if I am to understand this, you were more concerned with your own lives, than incurring my anger?'

The man straightened. 'We are men of Akri. We fear nothing, but to die without meat in our bellies, and gold in our hands.'

Korel closed his eyes. He hated this sort. Men who thought themselves above fear, above death. They were an odd sort to deal with, but he had found they could yet be persuaded.

'Khana...' Korel called, glancing behind him. Desert stretched back for kilometres, untouched. In the far distance, an outcropping of high, mountainous stones clawed at the sky. Beyond that, unseen, was the ancient city. Cursed lands to the Akrian people, especially the pirates.

His eyes moved away from the distant horizon, settling onto the form of a woman. She was slender, corded with muscle. She was wrapped here and there, with tight bands of sand coloured cloth, but her legs were exposed, and her feet bare.

'Master Korel?' She asked, stepping forward, a metal spear not dissimilar from Korel's held tightly in her hands.

'The gentleman seems to be under the impression that there is nothing to fear in death...'

The woman glanced across from her, to the only other man who stood with Korel, facing down the dozen Akrian pirates. 'There is only fear in death!' she said, turning back to face Korel.

'As I have taught, so you say,' he nodded. 'I pray you teach this man as I have taught you.'

'Master?'

'Send him to the dark one.'

There was silence. He turned more directly to her. She had stiffened. He hardened his gaze, his eyes burning into her. 'Khana... I have given you a command!'

The woman shook herself free of her thoughts, her fears, and nodded. She stepped forward, holding her spear aloft, levelling the tip towards Appuja. 'As you command, so I do.'

'Korel, please!' Appuja said, his eyes wild. 'I have done more! I have not failed you!'

Korel lifted a hand, and Khana stepped back, letting her spear drop to her side.

'More? Speak it now, Appuja, or you will learn what awaits you beyond this life. You will learn to believe in the old gods, as I have learned.'

The pirate swallowed. 'By your word, I speak!' he took a steadying breath, looking behind him, to his men. 'Serji!'

There was movement within the ranks, a small man, no taller than Korel's waist, bustled through the group to stand near Appuja. He bowed. 'Appuja!'

'Tell him! Tell him what I commanded of you... When we were met by the strong man!'

The little man bowed again, turning to Korel. He saw a dark glint in Serji's eyes as he ran a hand over his bald head. 'When we set against the man, Appuja didn't believe your words about him being more than a man. But still, I used a potion on them, and put

The Wishcharmer Saga: Beginnings

them in a great sleep. The power of my drink should have lasted for days, lord Korel... but they awoke in hours!'

'And this is when the battle broke out?'

'Yes, lord Korel.'

'And then, your Kilrot dead, you let them escape?'

The man bowed again. 'Let them away... But not escape!'

Korel narrowed his eyes against the little man. 'What do you mean?'

Serji smiled. 'Do you believe yourself to be the only one in favour of dark gods? I have served longer than most, lord Korel. My faith has given way to blessings...' he wrung his hands. 'Magics! The darkest kinds...'

Korel straightened. He looked on the little man, understanding dawning on him. Yes, he understood, but found himself confused. He knew the dark gods granted powers to their followers. Twisted magic, the likes the world had not known in eons. Still, he knew little of them. He had been tasked with different matters by his master.

Vance Smith

'What have you done, sir Serji?'

'An ancient spell...' He insisted, with a twisted smile. 'Darkness follows that man, lord Korel. You look to him, not knowing what he is, only knowing your master wants him. I look on him, with the eyes of the ancient gods, knowing him...'

'Then name him!' Korel insisted.

'Wishcharmer!' Serji smiled.

Korel twitched. 'Impossible!'

'Perhaps your master tells you little of your deeds? A Wishcharmer has been raised, to stop your master from awakening.' The little man raised his hands, patting the air to calm Korel's rising panic. If a Wishcharmer was still alive, if they could be called to cause, to stop the awakening...

'What dark spell have you worked?' Korel growled, levelling his spear on the little man.

Serji laughed. 'Fear! You fear to fail him... Serji wonders... What have you promised the dark one, in return for your position, for your power? I wonder, what is the price?'

'You spoke of service to the dark gods!' Korel

The Wishcharmer Saga: Beginnings

snapped. 'You spoke of knowing this Wishcharmer...
Then tell me, I say, what have you done to stop his
course?'

'Wayward Shadow!' Serji cackled.

18

There was a crack of thunder from somewhere in the blue sky. Will looked up, unable to understand where it had come from. He rested his hand on the hilt of the sword hanging at his hip.

'Did you hear that?' he asked, looking across the empty battlefield to Rajhu. The man shook his head, cocking an eyebrow. 'You're hearing things, now?'

Will sighed, looking back to the clear afternoon sky.

It had been hours since the battle with General

The Wishcharmer Saga: Beginnings

Val'kez. Still, Buri and the others were cleaning up after the mess that had been left behind. There were people moving about, peeking out of the large building, to see the aftermath of battle. Will knew most, if not all of the people that lived here had seen as much or more in their day. He didn't know how they felt about such things now, however.

'Raj, there was thunder. Just now, out of the blue sky.'

'Please...' Rajhu dragged a hand down his face, grumbling as he set his eyes on Will once more. 'No more adventure, Will... For one day, let's be done with it...'

'You're just going to ignore this?'

Rajhu furrowed his brow. He stepped forward, until he was no more than a pace from Will. Leaning in, he looked up, toward the heavens. His eyes lingered for a moment, before returning to Will. 'Yes.' He insisted, turning and hurrying away.

'Raj... Where are you going?' Will called.

'Away!' Rajhu snapped in response. 'Away from magic and men and Wishcharmers! I need to be alone!'

The man waved off Will's look of concern and headed away, wandering off to the right, toward an overgrown path that wound it's way past the huge home, and into the thick mountain forest.

Will watched Rajhu go, his eyes lingering on him as he went.

Something wasn't right.

As Rajhu walked away, Will could see a shadow lingering where it shouldn't have been. It hung off of the shadow of Rajhu's hand, too large and square to be a trick of the light. Will narrowed his eyes.

'What in the world...' he whispered, taking a step forward.

'Woah! Where you headed?'

Will looked up suddenly, his eyes met by a shirtless man with red hair. He didn't look to be much older than Will, if he was at all. It was this man who'd come to their aid in battle. It had been he who defeated Val'kez.

'Sorry?' Will asked, blinking.

'You look like you were confused by something!

The Wishcharmer Saga: Beginnings

I'm Rua, by the way... Cool sword!'

Will shook his head. 'Oh, thanks...'

'No problem!' Rua smiled. 'I'm good at pointing out stuff. You got pretty banged up, ya know. Are you and your friend okay?'

Will nodded absently, looking off into the trees. 'Yeah... That old lady patched us up pretty good.'

'Amazing!' he laughed. 'She can bring guys back from the brink of death, you know?'

Will didn't doubt it. He and Rajhu hadn't been in good shape when the battle had finally ended. Now he felt sore, but little else.

'So... that Rajhu is your friend?'

'Yeah... We've known each other for years. He's my best friend.'

'And a Wishcharmer...'

Will looked to the man. He nodded, not knowing what else to do. Buri had told Will that Rua was a Wishcharmer, and could help Rajhu learn to master his powers, but still... He didn't know this man. While Buri may trust him, Will had no reason to do likewise.

'Listen, I appreciate you coming in at the last

minute and saving our necks...'

'Hey, who doesn't like a good fight, right?'

Will smirked. 'Alright... I've gotta go find my friend, now. You'll excuse me?'

'Sure thing, man...'

Will nodded to the man and stepped past him. He started forward, veering toward the tree line. He needed to find Raj, to tell him about the strange shadow he had seen. The man wouldn't like it, but Will didn't have a good feeling. Something about that shadow was wrong, and he needed to get to the bottom of it. If he could find Rajhu, may be they could go ask Buri about it.

Will took a deep breath, settling into an easy pace. He walked on, divining on what that shadow could possibly mean. He felt his hand reach up, and wrap around the hilt of the Taintless Blade. An icy hot clarity poured through him, raging against every synapse. In a rush of motion, Buri flickered into existence before him. The man's form shook, distorting and shifting.

'Will! Rajhu... Wayward Shadow!'

The Wishcharmer Saga: Beginnings

With no explanation, the man vanished once more and Will stumbled through the spot where the visage of the man had stood. Gasping, Will pulled his hand away from the sword, looking around, his whole body aching from the act.

'Wh-' Will gasped again. 'Wayward Shadow?' he echoed aloud, looking around. 'What is that supposed to mean?' he shouted, looking around. He grabbed the hilt of the Taintless Blade again, but nothing happened as his flesh brushed the soft cloth wrappings.

'Woah... You talk to your sword, too?' Rua asked, walking up and standing beside Will. 'You're a pretty crazy guy, you know?'

Will straightened, pushing past Rua. 'I'm sorry, I don't have time to talk right now... I... I need to find Raj!' He started away again.

'I guess you're right!' Rua said. 'If there's a Wayward Shadow around here... then we're all in big trouble...'

Will stopped in his tracks. He felt a shiver of fear crawling up his spine as he turned to face the young

Vance Smith

Wishcharmer. He man stood, placid, with his hands in the pockets of his tattered pants.

'You know what a Wayward Shadow is?' Will asked.

Rua shrugged. 'Doesn't everyone?'

Will shook his head. 'You don't understand me. I *need* to know. Rua, what is a Wayward Shadow?'

The Wishcharmer sighed, his head drooping for a moment. Pain washed over his features before settling into a steely look of resignation.

'Djinn magic... Some of their most powerful. I've only come across them once before... But they're dangerous.'

'How dangerous?' Will pressed.

'The worst.' Rua breathes. 'They're little worlds, attached to people, and filled with creatures of the Djinn's own making. They call them Shadelings... But that's not the worst part...'

'What do you mean?'

'Well, lots of things... But what should concern you right now is... they were created specifically to kill Wishcharmers...'

The Wishcharmer Saga: Beginnings

Will felt as though the ground had dropped out from under him. He turned to the distant tree line, his eyes darting here and there.

'Oh no... Rajhu...' He whispered.

Vance Smith

19

A cool breeze sifted through the needles of the evergreens, bending the tall grass that hugged the winding pathway. Rajhu turned his face into the wind, letting it caress his cuts, the cold of it soothing him.

He supposed he should be grateful. While Val'Kez had torn him and Will apart, one of the ancient women of the retirement home had put them back together. Rajhu swatted at the tall grass and cursed. Was it so much to ask that they needn't require repairing in the first place?

'Lords above, how did I ever get involved with this in the first place?' Raj grumbled, looking up, through the canopy of trees. 'Am I not a good person?'

Wind rushed against him, colder than before. Raj turned from the gale and simpered. 'So I am not perfect!'

He looked down at his hands, remembering the things he had done, not just this day, but every day since the market. Since he had taken that cursed lamp, since his life had fallen hopelessly apart.

'If my greed be a problem, why did you give it to me in the first place?' he growled, looking up again. 'I gave back the lamp! Why do you punish me in this way? Is it not extreme?'

No reply fell from the heavens, and so Raj swatted at the tall grass again, pulling the heads of the stocks off and tossing them on the ground. They scattered across the dry dirt path, a splash of colour against a river of blacks and browns. He sighed, and started forward, following the path deeper as it wound its way down a steep hill. In the distance he could hear the babbling of moving water. Ahead, near the base of the hill, Rajhu could see the snaking shape of an easily flowing creek. It looked deep in places, and inviting. Suddenly Raj became aware of his parched throat. He wondered at the sweetness of the cold stream, and how it would feel to taste of it, and to soothe his wounds with it's frigid touch.

He started forward again, in earnest. Every step he took, he felt himself growing more and more thirsty.

'Koliba! I need a drink!' he mumbled, quickening his pace.

Something brushed his right hand, making him pull it back, looking about. Rajhu prayed it wasn't a large mountain bug. He hated bugs! As he looked around, seeing nothing, he wondered if the mountains even had bugs. Will had once told him that the northern countries had few insects, and those that did live there, were dwarfed by their southern counterparts. He didn't know if it were true, or just another wild tale from the boy.

He took a deep breath, filling his lungs with the

The Wishcharmer Saga: Beginnings

sweet mountain air. If anything, he would miss that, when he left.

Sunlight dappled through the treetops, falling across him in patches of light and shadow. Still, the warmth of the sun reached him easily, melting away his insecurities.

'You are beginning to lose it, Rajhu... Breathe... Think!'

He moved forward, passing under the shadow of a large tree. For a moment, it blocked out the sun, sending a chill over Raj. When he stepped back into the light of the high sun, he felt something brush his hand again. Rajhu looked down in an instant, his eyes falling onto his own shadow. About his hand, he saw something queer, something that shouldn't have been. A shadow clung to him, as if it were his own, but he knew it wasn't. It couldn't be.

Square, and nearly the size of a suitcase, the shadow hung against the ground, against him. Then, in a rush, it opened.

Rajhu jumped back as a wisp of darkness snaked free of the shadow and lunged at him as it solidified.

Vance Smith

Teeth and claws reached for him, and Rajhu pitched backward, losing his balance. The earth came up to meet him as the world spun. Aware he was tumbling down the path, Rajhu flung out his arms, digging his hands into the gravel path. He felt skin tear, but he slowed, finally coming to a stop.

Breathing wildly, Rajhu looked up. For a moment, he saw nothing. A sound like the cawing of a bird drew his eyes to a dark form of smooth, sharp angles. The monster hung from the side of a large evergreen, red eyes burning into Rajhu's core. He had never seen a monster like this. To Raj, it seemed a cross between a lizard of some kind, and an obsidian beetle. A flat face held vaguely human shapes, but they were distorted, and vile. It's head was clean and bald and smooth. When it opened it's mouth, it let out a harsh caw, sharp teeth visible even from where Rajhu lay.

The beast bounded from the side of the tree, soaring through the air. It clasped the thick trunk of another evergreen before launching itself directly at Raj.

Scrambling to his feet, Raju lifted his scraped,

The Wishcharmer Saga: Beginnings

bleeding arms. Blue light sifted from his flesh, growing and solidifying as the monster reached him. Arms of shifting light met the obsidian beast. Blue claws broke the shell-like flesh. Rajhu brought the arms down, crushing the beast into the path. It squirmed for a moment, then fell still. Rajhu stumbled, falling against a tree. Breathing heavily, he looked around, but saw no more of the creatures.

'By heavens...' he whispered. 'What was *that?*'

Running a hand over his face, Rajhu straightened. He needed to get back to the retirement home. There, maybe Will or Buri could tell him...

Rajhu looked down, and the shadow opened.

'Oh, koliba!' he cursed.

Five forms jumped free of the shadow, then ten, then twenty! Rajhu backed off the path, looking for an escape. The forms solidified, closing in on him. Raj turned, but his foot caught in the undergrowth. He pitched forward, falling into the wet moss. He rolled onto his back as one of the monsters came to stand over him. The thing had no lips, and this close, Rajhu could see that it wasn't shell, but flesh that covered the beast. It opened it's mouth, it's jaw unhinging. Large pincers slid free from fleshy pockets in the side of it's throat as the thing let out a guttural howl.

Raj stared wide eyed at the beast.

This was the end.

A sword cleaved the head of the monster in half. Blood spit from the sundered flesh, falling against Raj, burning lightly. The creature gargled, struggling against the wound, before falling dead at Rajhu's feet. Will stood above him, Taintless Blade in hand.

'Oh, thank the Powers!' Rajhu sighed.

'Get up, Raj!' Will commanded, turning as another of the monsters came at him. Raj climbed to his feet as Will moved this way and that, dodging the creature's attacks with an unnatural grace. He sunk below a swipe of the beast's claws, stepping forward and impaling it with the sword, against a tree.

Three more monsters rushed at Raj and Will. They were half way to them, when a screaming man dashed through the trees, jumping in the way. He ducked under the first attack, an arm reaching out and grabbing the monster by the throat. He threw it into the distance as the other two bore down on him.

Blue light surged across the shirtless man's flesh and he let out a scream of rage as he stepped forward, his fist crashing into the first, it's head flying off it's body. Blood sprayed across his chest, burning into the flesh, but he moved again, grabbing the next monster about the shoulders, slamming his head into it's chest. The arms of the monster ripped from it as it sailed away, crashing through a tree. The evergreen toppled, falling in a rush and crushing nearly a dozen of the beasts.

'Go!' the man screamed, as more of the monsters scrambled forward.

'Where the blazes are we supposed to go?' Raj asked, turning as one of the black monsters descended on him. Blue arms of shifting light burst from his back. Fists formed. Raj punched, the impact bursting the creature apart.

Will swung, cleaving another of the creatures in two.

'What are they?' Raj asked.

Vance Smith

'Shadelings!' Will grunted, pinning one of the beasts to the ground with his sword. Breathing heavily, Will pulled his sword free, looking across the underbrush to Raj. Blood stained much of the greenery.

'Is that all of them?'

'I think so...' Will sighed.

'Not quite...' the shirtless man growled. He turned, facing Rajhu, his face awash with rage. Dark blood covered him, his flesh red from it's burning. He stalked forward, moving toward Raj, who looked to Will for some kind of explanation. When none came, he looked to the man, but it was too late. A fist swung, cracking against Rajhu's arm. Pain shot through him and he stumbled to a knee.

'What the devil are you doing?' Raj demanded.

'Quiet!' the man growled, looking up as the sunlight filtered through the trees, falling across Raj.

The man's hand shot forward. Raj tried to move, but it was too late. One hand grabbed him about the shoulder, holding him fast, while the other reached into the shadow that clung to him. The man pitched

The Wishcharmer Saga: Beginnings

forward, sinking through nothing, down to his shoulder. He struggled, growling. Finally, in a rush, he launched himself backward.

Raj saw the man crash down, into the underbrush. Something had come with him out of the shadow. Raj scrambled back, his eyes falling onto the beautiful form of a young girl. She couldn't have been much older than Will or the shirtless boy.

'Who is she?' he asked, but the boy gave no answer. The girl struggled against him, snarling and spitting. She lashed against him with clawed hands, but he forced his way past the attacks. He grabbed her wrists, pinning her to the ground and sitting on her.

'Stop struggling!' he growled.

'Will, what is all of this?' Rajhu wondered.

He shook his head. 'I... I don't know...'

'Stop the attack!' the shirtless boy growled.

'Never!' the girl screamed. 'I must... kill the Wishcharmer!'

'Rua, who is she?'

The shirtless boy didn't answer Will. His eyes were

locked on the struggling girl. 'Stop this, or I will stop you!' Rua shouted.

'I *can't!*' the girl screamed.

Rua grabbed her wrists tighter, squeezing them in his grip. Blue mist enveloped his hands, her wrists, and the girl screamed.

'What are you doing?' Rajhu called, moving toward the boy.

'Stay back!' Rua growled, over the scream of the woman. She arched her back, the sound of her anguish echoing through the forest as it died on her lips.

Rua pulled his hands away. Where they had been, heavy brass bracers now covered the girl's wrists, a few limp links of chain hanging from each, connecting to nothing.

Slowly, Rua moved back, lifting the girl into his arms. He looked across her to Raj. 'You must be scaring all the wrong people, mister... They locked a Wayward Shadow to you...'

'What is that?' Raj asked. 'Who is she?'

'Her?' Rua asked, looking down on the girl in his

arms. He took a slow breath, looking back to Raj. 'She's the one they sent to kill you.'

'Who?' Will wondered.

Rua shrugged. 'Whoever wants to kill the Wishcharmers.'

'What are you talking about?' Rajhu asked. 'I don't understand any of this!'

'I don't understand much of it either,' Rua admitted. 'This girl... she's a Shadeling. She's a victim in all this, just like you.'

'How is that?' Will scoffed. 'She tried to kill us!'

Rua shook his head. 'There's too much to try and explain here. Besides, Buri knows better than me. Help me bring her back to the house. I'll explain everything there.'

'She tried to kill us!' Will insisted. 'You want to bring her with us?'

'Of course!' Rua said, forcing a smile. 'She can help save all of us... If we can save her...'

Rajhu let his head fall. Things were getting complicated...

Made in the USA
Charleston, SC
22 October 2016